T0017818

ROANOKE

RIDGE

CREATURE X MYSTERIES

Roanoke Ridge

J.J. DUPUIS

ROANOKE

RIDGE

A CREATURE X MYSTERY

DUNDURN

TORONTO

Publisher: Scott Fraser | Acquiring editor: Scott Fraser | Editor: Allison Hirst
Cover designer: Laura Boyle
Cover image: istockphoto.com/valio84sl
Printer: Marquis Book Printing Inc.

Library and Archives Canada Cataloguing in Publication

Title: Roanoke Ridge / J.J. Dupuis.
Names: Dupuis, J. J., 1983- author.
Description: Series statement: A Creature X mystery
Identifiers: Canadiana (print) 2019023167X | Canadiana (ebook) 20190231688 |
  ISBN 9781459746459
  (softcover) | ISBN 9781459746466 (PDF) | ISBN 9781459746473 (EPUB)
Classification: LCC PS8607.U675 R63 2020 | DDC C813/.6—dc23

We acknowledge the support of the Canada Council for the Arts and the Ontario Arts Council for our publishing program. We also acknowledge the financial support of the Government of Ontario, through the Ontario Book Publishing Tax Credit and Ontario Creates, and the Government of Canada.

Care has been taken to trace the ownership of copyright material used in this book. The author and the publisher welcome any information enabling them to rectify any references or credits in subsequent editions.

The publisher is not responsible for websites or their content unless they are owned by the publisher.

Printed and bound in Canada.

VISIT US AT

 dundurn.com | @dundurnpress | dundurnpress | dundurnpress

Dundurn
3 Church Street, Suite 500
Toronto, Ontario, Canada
M5E 1M2

I know I won't be able to convince the world by argument, because it doesn't want to be convinced. I just keep going — and I will do — until one of these creatures is collected dead or alive.

— René Dahinden

PROLOGUE

FOR THE FIRST TIME IN MY LIFE, I SEE A wounded Sasquatch running straight into a crowd of people holding cotton candy. It has a head start, but it's hurt, cradling its left arm. My friend — well, best friend, I guess — Saad is behind me, trying to capture the whole thing on his cellphone camera. I know, I just know that the video will be one long blur and I may as well be chasing Santa Claus. It'll never hold up, definitely not in a court of law. Saad breathes heavily, his feet slap on the concrete. I feel better knowing he's there.

The air is hot and thick with the smell of burgers and hot dogs cooking on a half-dozen barbecues. The Sasquatch turns a corner and almost knocks over a little boy with a snow cone. There's a parade happening and the main street of the town is shut down. I keep pace and even gain on the furry ape-man as he runs right across the street, between floats and into a curious crowd. I run in front of an old black convertible with a trio of silver-haired women from the Ladies' Auxiliary who are throwing packets of candy into the crowd. Behind the wheel is a fat old guy with dark Elvis-style sunglasses. He honks at me, but I keep running.

There's no question of primate locomotion here, bipedalism versus brachiation versus quadrapedalism. It's just running, running for its life. Sasquatch runs behind the drugstore, down a side street that slopes down into a parking lot. It's opened up its wound — I can see the blood.

"Stop!" I yell.

It's a beautiful day. A wall of evergreen trees rises up behind the Sasquatch, just across the river. This whole town is like paradise, nestled among mountains and river valleys. But it's not beautiful enough to erase death.

ONE

What did startle him, however, was that these footprints were of a naked foot of a distinctly human shape and proportion but, by actual measurement, a whopping 16 inches long!

— Ivan T. Sanderson, "The Story of America's Abominable Snowman," *True*, 1969

THERE IS NOTHING OUT HERE BUT TREES. No restaurants or gas stations. Just trees on either side of the highway, broken up by the odd rocky outcropping or pond filled with cattails and floating logs. In the distance, far from any roads or trails, I can see pristine old-growth patches of western hemlock and Douglas fir.

The radio is on. Some kind of folk music plays between static crackles. Saad isn't listening to it; neither am I. We're not talking. Maybe we used up all the conversation on the flight from Cleveland. We flew into Sacramento this morning instead of Portland because it's closer, and we wouldn't have to wait another day until the next flight into Medford.

Saad keeps his back perfectly straight and stares straight ahead. As each minute of silence passes, it feels more and more like I should have left him at home. This is not his problem. Sometimes it feels like Saad's life is all mapped out for him and I just screw with that plan, because I'm selfish or stupid. It's another detour for him, like the conferences or the speaking appearances, all the extras that come with running a popular website. And he's been there, like a rock, from the very beginning.

I distract myself by thinking of all the thousands of people who followed this same trail westward, looking to cash in on the bounty of natural resources cached away in the mountains of the Pacific Northwest — the loggers, the miners. Hordes of people, mainly men, trying their luck in a land with less order, less structure, and less scrutiny than the cities back east. The teeming wilderness conjures up both a sense of freedom and a desire to exploit, to take or name that which belongs to no one else.

Turning off Interstate 5, we come to a detour. Two inches of rain fell last night, causing both a landslide and a sinkhole to open up in the middle of Old Highway 99. A highway patrolman redirects us down a quiet road. The patrolman's uniform, its two shades of blue like the cop in Norman Rockwell's *The Runaway*, tells me we've crossed the state line into Oregon, the khaki-coloured California cops I know from reruns of *CHiPs* now behind us. Birds of prey, perched on bare trees, watch us as we pass.

"I can take over the driving, if you want," I say.

"I'm fine," Saad says.

"Twenty percent of this state is either Forest Service or Bureau of Land Management property, did you know that?"

Saad shakes his head, keeping his eyes locked on the road ahead. The sun hangs low in the sky, ducking behind the pointed tops of pine trees. A minivan with two canoes on the roof rack drives toward us, passes with a whooshing sound. Saad looks like he desperately wants to talk about something, but won't. He adjusts his grip on the steering wheel, tightening it and then relaxing it. He swallows and I watch his Adam's apple move. He's too logical, too analytical to get hung up like this. I'm trying not to watch, but I almost enjoy it.

"Laura," he says, turning his face a little toward me but keeping his eyes on the road. "You didn't ..."

"Didn't what?"

"You and the professor ... did you ...?"

"Sleep with Professor Sorel? No!" I say, relieved that he finally spoke.

"It's just — we're travelling halfway across the country for a man who taught you for only two semesters, six years ago."

"I know. Weird, right? But there are those professors, those mentors, who you meet at just the right time, just when you need them, and they profoundly change you. They change your life. I wouldn't be doing what I do now, there wouldn't be a website, if it weren't for Professor Sorel."

There's a lie in there, if lies by omission are really a thing. But not the one Saad was suspecting. I don't feel as if Saad would judge me, or my family; he's not that type of guy. There are just certain things that I decided years ago, before I even met him, that I would not talk about. I can't change the past, but I can control the narrative. If I don't breathe the words into existence they are less real.

This part of Oregon is littered with rivers and ghost towns, volcanic lakes and mountain ranges. I can see myself retiring out here in forty years, maybe buying a cabin much sooner than that. Saad breathes in the mountain air that pours through his window and I find there's a part of me that is really, really hoping he enjoys it.

The little satellite dish icon in the top corner of my phone screen stands by itself, abandoned by reception bars. I feel liberated, free of cell service, free of Wi-Fi, even the car's radio fades out into nothing but crackles.

The highway stretches before us and winds through tree-covered mountains. Beyond them are miles of rugged country, backstopped by the Pacific Ocean. This whole area is dotted with logging camps — Oregon has been called "The Timber Queen of the United States" — and every few miles, we come to turnoffs that lead into the trees, logging roads that cut through the forest. Trucks carrying timber roar past us.

My clever little shortcut was for naught. The detour forces us to move like a boomerang, adds another forty-five minutes to our journey. We drive north, then curve back down toward Roanoke Valley, as though we came in from Portland. We don't see anybody else on the road until we get close to town.

"I forgot how much I missed this. Greenery as far as the eye can see," I say. "I miss it so much, I find myself spending hours staring out my bedroom window toward the tiny patch of wetland on the other side of the train tracks, watching for any bird larger than a gull to fly by."

"Maybe you'll miss the city after a few days out here," Saad says.

"Not likely."

We pull off the highway into a gravel parking lot nestled among the evergreen trees. A man-sized bear carved out of wood stands guard over the Tall Pines Motel, a long, single-storey building that mixes Tudor-style design with Pacific Northwest kitsch. A rack of moose antlers is bolted over the door to the office. There's a sign in the window that reads NO VACANCY in neon green lights, the NO unlit and barely visible from the mouth of the driveway.

Attached to the back of the office is a bungalow where I assume the proprietor lives. It has an extra half storey on top with a satellite dish growing out the side of it like fungus. What a quaint way to live. If not for my feeling that car culture is going extinct, I can almost see myself running a little motel like this by a highway somewhere. I'm just happy that the management here doesn't live in a big, creepy old Victorian house on a hill behind the place. I wonder if there've been any studies on the amount of business that Alfred Hitchcock cost the motel industry in the U.S. after the release of *Psycho*.

The busy tourist season is still about a month away, but the annual Roanoke Valley Bigfoot Festival is kicking off now, and there are only three spots left at the far end of the parking lot, in the shade of the tall pines that must have given the motel its name. The rest of the lot is filled with pickup trucks, vans, and SUVs. Our rental is the only compact car. It's also the only foreign car, except for a silver Subaru Outback that shines in the sun.

Saad moves toward the office with a hurried determination, as though someone may pop out of one of these parked cars and beat him to the last available suites. I text Barbara, Professor Sorel's wife, to tell her we've arrived. Aunt Barb is staying at the Golden Eagle Motel, which the NatureWorld network has rented for the cast and crew of *The Million Dollar Bigfoot Hunt*, the show Professor Sorel was involved with when he disappeared.

There's a freshness in the air that I wish I could bottle up and take with me everywhere. Maybe it's psychological, the effect of seeing the tall pines and the mountains behind the motel, tree-crested ridges in every direction. Maybe it's the lack of visible industry — no smoke stacks, no factories, no smog. It could be nostalgia, the sweet memories of my childhood spent in these mountains.

I hurry across the parking lot, feeling the gravel and stones through the thin soles of my sneakers. Saad is at the office door, pulling it wide and waiting for me to enter. In the bottom corner of the door I see two words that bring both joy and anxiety: *Free Wi-Fi*. No escape from work after all.

The office is dark inside. A lingering smell of oak makes the place feel like home, like the cottages and cabins of my childhood. The pelt of a black bear stretches across the wall behind the front desk, its sheen lost under a faint layer of grey dust. The entire room is wood panelled; if you squint hard enough you can see sheets of plastic in the gaps between the boards. In front of the desk is a rack of pamphlets featuring various local attractions from all the way up and down the Pacific coast. On the wall, next to an alcove filled with various knick-knacks, sits a signboard with a marmot wearing a forest ranger hat. A word bubble leading out of the rodent's mouth says *Check out our gift shop!* There are piles of T-shirts, a few books, photographs, and postcards, as well as various mason jars filled with preserves.

"GPS not working?" the bald, plaid-shirt-wearing manager says as Saad approaches him.

"We're exactly where we're supposed to be," I say.

"We'd like two suites, please," Saad says.

A smile appears on the manager's face. His shoulders relax. He now has a stake in the game.

"Alls we got is a double suite, and that's only because we just got a cancellation. That's one room, two double beds."

Saad turns to me, his mouth hanging open a bit. I nod at him. At this point, we'll take what we can get. He hesitates, still quiet, then moves closer to the counter.

The manager slides the register over toward him, across the glass counter that has a map underneath.

"I thought you folks were lost," he says. "We get a lot of young people passing through here, driving between San Francisco and Seattle or Vancouver."

"An honest mistake," I say.

"You don't look like squatchers," he says.

"We're not."

"Name's Clive," he says. "Anything you need, you just let me know."

We take some time to fill out the paper register, then Clive takes our credit card information. He unhooks the last, lonely keychain from the wall. The key is attached to a slat of wood with the room number burned into it, like something a freshman makes in shop class.

Saad leads me back out, pushing the door open and letting the sunlight in. On the way out, I notice the bulletin board to the left of the door, plastered with flyers and business cards. The top sheet, prominent in the centre of the board and printed on bright green paper, is a notice for a lecture on the distribution of Sasquatch in the northwest. It's tonight, eight thirty, at the Roanoke Valley Rotary Club. The speaker is a grad student from Washington State University. Her name seems strangely familiar.

Saad takes all the bags out of the trunk: his suitcase and laptop bag, my duffel bag with my laptop inside. I unlock the motel room door and push it wide open, ushering Saad in. He walks inside and pauses midway, his arm going slack on the handle of his suitcase as he looks around the room, breathes in the smell left behind by the ozone generator used to cleanse the air combined with the pine scent used to mask it. His eyes linger over the TV with the bulging, cathode tube–filled rear.

I rewind through memories of a hundred highway-side motels just like this one, family road trips with the windows down and oldies playing. How many rainy afternoons did I spend on the edge of beds like these ones, watching movies starring animals, like *Beethoven* or *Free Willy*, Mom crocheting, glancing out the window, waiting for the rain to stop?

The ringing of my cellphone, deep in my purse, brings me back to the present. Barbara Sorel is already here, in the parking lot. I'm surprised and thankful that I get reception out here.

I peel the door back and Aunt Barb seems frozen on the sill. Saad nods and waves from across the room, and I make a quick introduction. Her plump, lined face is haggard. She breathes heavily and tugs at the bottom of her yellow raincoat. We hug, then I offer her a seat and a glass of water. She holds the plastic cup like a praying Buddhist holds incense, her pale skin drawn tight over her long, bony fingers.

"I'm so happy you came, dear," she says.

"How could I not?" I say. "I want to help in any way I can."

She rocks back and forth in her chair, looking into her cup like there's a cue card floating inside with her next line. "I told Berton he was too old to go off in the woods by himself, and know what he told me? He said, 'Barb, you're rushing me into an early grave.' Now look where we are."

Her voice is a little stronger than when she called last night, sobbing. There are still cracks in it, signs of exhaustion, but she is focused now. The worry is gone for the moment. It will come back, though, when everything is quiet and she stops moving.

"Professor Sorel is tough. He's a skilled outdoorsman. Most importantly, he's a survivor."

Professor Sorel is not the feeble bookworm you might expect from an academic. Sure, he's old, but he's wiry and tough. I took a summer class with him once. He'd show up in a T-shirt, swollen veins rappelling down his defined biceps, and I could see the amazement on the faces of the boys in the class, boys who spent time in the weight room on campus trying to pump up, boys who didn't know the difference between size and strength. He grew up out here among the mountains, where hunting, fishing, and trapping used to be a way of life, not a weekend activity, and he and Aunt Barb still live in a cabin an hour north of here, a straight shot up the highway. He's the kind of man who chops wood to heat his home in the winter.

The sky opens and rain pours down slowly and steadily. The weather is prone to its moods just like the rest of us — it'll stop when it damn well feels like it. The raindrops hitting the gravel outside sound like slow-moving maracas. Such is the Pacific Northwest: a swath of damp earth spanning two countries, sandwiched between mountains and an ocean, with rain like London.

Aunt Barb turns and looks through the part in the curtains, to the rain falling in the parking lot. Her profile shows her age, her worry. The gravity of her missing husband presses down hard on her shoulders. I can't help but wonder if there's more to it than that, if it's not just this one crisis, but the life of potential crises that her husband's obsession brings with it. Professor Sorel ducks ridicule from his fellow academics like a champion boxer slips punches. But he isn't comfortable just flying below the radar. He releases his papers online and defies his peers to poke holes in his research. He haunts talk radio studios at every opportunity, has become the butt of jokes on call-in shows that stretched through the night.

"When was the last time you ate, Aunt Barb?"

"I had a doughnut and a coffee at the ranger station this morning," she says.

All I have left from my road trip snacks are a granola bar and a bag of dried mangoes. I offer both to Aunt Barb, who waves at them and shakes her head. She pinches her eyes closed and the skin on her face folds inward.

"If I never see any more granola …"

"You've got to eat something."

"I … I can't …"

"Let's go into town and get something hot."

We stand up in unison, slowly. Her perfume makes the jump across the carpet, and it smells stronger to me than it did when I hugged her.

Saad is unzipping each of the hundred pockets on his suitcase. His laptop and its power cord are already on the nightstand, and his contact lens solution and the case the lenses come in are on the little table between the bed and the bathroom.

"Saad, want to go into town?" I ask.

All the unzipping noises stop, and the bedsprings creak as he stands up. He takes a bright orange rain slicker out of his suitcase, slides it over his head, then opens his umbrella and waits for Aunt Barb, walking her out through the rain like she is the First Lady. Saad turns to perform the same service for me, but I'm already at the car, raindrops tapping on the bill of my baseball cap.

We drive down moss-banked roads under a grey sky. It's not hard to believe that the trees and rocks out here hide a large primate who watches from the woods, its massive feet sinking into the damp earth. Bigfoot, for many, is the face of the unknown, the manifestation of a million miles of wilderness, of every cave and creek where people have never set foot.

As we get closer to the centre of town, driveways and storefronts increasingly interrupt the trees. There's a tavern, a bait-and-tackle shop, and a place advertising wood furniture, carvings, and "authentic Indian" arts and crafts. Roanoke Village proper is pretty much just a crucifix on the land: a long strip of old one- and two-storey shops, bisected by a shorter strip with more of the same. Saad parks the car between two trucks by the curb on the main street, right in front of the open sign of Shirley's Bigfoot Diner — née Shirley's Diner, before the Bigfoot craze took hold.

Inside the diner, a few feet from the front door, is a wraparound glass counter filled with baked goods, sandwiches and bagels, juice bottles and pop cans, even jars of honey made locally. It's L-shaped and stretches all the way toward the back wall. The walls and ceiling are panelled with wood. The clock on the wall has the Pepsi logo on it. On the pillar holding up the back of the diner is a poster showing all the fish species native to the local waters.

A heavy-set waitress, her blond hair escaping her dark roots, tells us to grab a seat anywhere we'd like, and promises to be with us in a "sec." We take a booth next to a poster that reads *Fish Oregon Waters … Drive Oregon Highways*. There's an illustration of a man in hip waders with a salmon on the end of his fly-fishing line, while his wife waits patiently by the passenger door of their 1940 Chevrolet Special Deluxe sedan.

We start with three cups of coffee. I drink mine black; I have ever since I was a little girl, on camping trips with my dad, when he'd boil a blue, enamel kettle over the fire and pour two cups of the nastiest instant coffee for us. I've heard other people reminisce about their fathers letting them take a sip of beer from them while watching Sunday football, or even whisky after dinner — but sharing that gross coffee, that was some serious bonding.

Aunt Barb warms her hands on a cup of coffee, empty creamers scattered between us. How many leaning towers or pyramids have I made out of creamers on tables just like this? She lets the rising steam warm her face. "I couldn't sit there waiting around that ranger station a second longer. I've never felt so helpless in all my life," Aunt Barb says.

The door chime rings and a pair of men dressed like hunters walk in. The rain continues to fall, and I try not to think about it washing Professor Sorel's footprints away, making it difficult for the search party to track him. My dad taught me about tracking not far from here, on day trips up the mountain. The terrain of the Cascade and Klamath Mountains offers lots of challenges to even the most experienced tracker, and the rain certainly doesn't help.

"Professor Sorel knows how to pack for this kind of expedition," I say. "He has at least two days' worth of food, a first aid kit, waterproof matches, and a thermal blanket. He'll be fine."

Aunt Barb leans across the table. Her eyes follow Saad as he walks to the washrooms at the back of the diner, past the curved glass display case displaying cakes, pies, tarts and brownies. "Berton didn't take his meds with him," she whispers.

"His meds?"

Aunt Barb reaches into her purse and gives me a pill bottle, concealing the label as she passes it to me. Sensing her privacy concerns, I hold the pill bottle just above my lap, squinting to read the small print. I expected pills for his heart or perhaps diabetes. The word *Risperidone* stands out as if written in neon.

"Professor Sorel is schizophrenic?" I say, just loud enough for Aunt Barb to hear.

She looks down at the Formica tabletop and nods.

"Does the search party know about this?"

Aunt Barb shakes her head. "Nobody knows except Berton, his doctor, me, and now you. He's worked so hard to maintain his credibility. His colleagues already mock him; if his struggles with mental illness become public knowledge, his career is over."

I once asked Professor Sorel if he was ever afraid of people thinking he was a kook. He smiled, leaned back in his chair, lacing his fingers behind his head, and stared up at the ceiling.

What really keeps me up at night, he'd said, *is the thought that I'll die, a coronary or stroke or something, maybe just peacefully in my sleep, and then a year or two down the road someone finds a Sasquatch finger, or a femur, not even a whole body, just a decaying piece of meat and bone. Just a hiker or climber, who just happened to be in the right place at the right time. That's what really scares me — the idea that my time will run out before then.*

I roll the pill bottle around to read the label more carefully. I check the date it was filled and the prescribed dosage. I open the lid, shake the bottle until all the pills are flat against the side, do a quick count, then do the math in my head.

"At least he brought some extra with him," I say.

"Nobody's more careful than Berton," Aunt Barb says. "But sometimes that scares me more. Lots of harmless things can cause a careless person to get lost. But a careful man …"

Aunt Barb's eyes flash as she looks toward the back of the diner. I turn and see Saad walking back to our table, his eyes lingering on a pie in the display case. I palm the pills back to Aunt Barb instinctively and immediately feel guilty. I know I can trust Saad, but it's not my secret to tell.

"That silly reality show was to start taping next week," Aunt Barb says. "*The Million Dollar Bigfoot Hunt*. Berton wanted to do some preliminary scouting. He told me he was going to where your father filmed those two Sasquatches."

"I'm confused," Saad said quietly, looking from me to Aunt Barb and back again.

"In the world of Bigfoot research," I say, "there are two films of the creature that have so far stood up to scrutiny, or at least can't be easily dismissed. The Patterson-Gimlin film, and the Roanoke Ridge film, which was shot close to twenty years ago. By my dad."

Saad raises his eyebrows, leaning back slightly as if to get a better look at me.

"Only a handful of people knew exactly where that video was shot, and only two of those people are still around. Professor Sorel and myself," I say. "I didn't meet Professor Sorel when I was in college. I've known him for most of my life."

"Only, Berton doesn't remember where the video was shot," Aunt Barb says. "At least, I don't think he's sure anymore."

"But my dad took him to the spot a few times."

"He certainly did, I remember it clearly. And Berton was up there, oh, just three years ago, setting camera traps. But two nights ago, I brought him his evening tea and found him poring over maps of the area. Laura, there were maps scattered all over his study. Topographical maps, BLM prospecting maps, maps drawn up by the Army Corps of Engineers. I asked him about the maps, and he said that they were part of his work, preparing for this reality show. I was ready to believe him, but then he pulled me down onto his lap and put his arms around me. Let's just say Berton got out of that habit before the kids went to college. But he held me tight like we were newlyweds and said, 'No matter what, we're going to be all right.'"

Aunt Barb wipes a tear away with the side of her index finger. I reach over to the shiny stainless steel napkin dispenser, pluck a few out, and pass them to her. She takes a few deep breaths, looking down at the tabletop. The chimes above the door ring and a man walks in wearing a T-shirt with an image of Bigfoot and the words *Bigfoot saw me but nobody believes him* written down the front.

"When the producers of *The Million Dollar Bigfoot Hunt* approached Berton, he was only supposed to be a judge, with Dr. Duncan Laidlaw and some other fellow. But Berton pushed the producers for a bigger role. He wanted a chance to win that prize money."

"He's never been the greedy type," I say.

"It's for his project. Unmanned aerial vehicles or some such. He's become obsessed with it."

"He wants to use drones to search for Bigfoot?" Saad asks, his brown eyes wide with incredulity.

"If a population of Sasquatches still exists today, it would have to be in territory that is both vast and remote, like the B.C. interior — a place that is still largely untouched by humans, even today," I say.

"He hoped to raise enough money to have a drone built with an infrared camera, so they could track animals through thick tree cover," Aunt Barb adds.

"I remember the Kickstarter campaign," I say.

"It never got off the ground," Aunt Barb says. "So he convinced the producer, Danny LeDoux, to let him compete for the prize. That only escalated things. This LeDoux fellow thought that Berton had a tremendous advantage, given his field experience, so he made sure to bring in serious competition. There's this big game hunter from Australia, and several of the top Bigfoot enthusiasts from North America. Even that con man Rick Driver was approached to compete."

"Anything for higher ratings," I say. "What do you expect from the channel that marketed a mermaid movie as a 'documentary'?" I turn to Saad, who is lacking in

Bigfoot context at the moment. "Rick Driver is a no-torious hoaxer, known for claiming to have a dead Bigfoot in his freezer."

"Please don't associate my husband with such men," Aunt Barb says to Saad pleadingly.

"Don't worry, he won't," I say. "Saad just finished his master's degree in chemical engineering. He knows the difference between hard science and pseudoscience. Not to mention flim-flam artists like Rick Driver."

"I'd like to think so," Saad says.

I think of the stories Saad's told me about all the con men in his native Pakistan, ones who use Islam the way faith healers here use Christianity to try and make a buck off the devout. He may be a stranger to our monsters, but he is no stranger to monsters in general. From what I've heard, there are as many folk creatures in Pakistan, the djinn, for example, as there are here. Many predate Islam and never seem to go away, even though the Qur'an doesn't seem to have room for them. Like how the Bible tried to eliminate the fairies and ogres that have persisted in European cultures past the onset of Christianity. The more I learn about Saad's home, the more it seems like people are the same everywhere.

"I'm so exhausted, dear," Aunt Barb says. "I'm just so exhausted." Her forearms slide back along the tabletop toward her body, ready to fall into her lap.

"We'll take you back to your motel so that you can rest," I say.

* * *

A few minutes later, Saad sits behind the steering wheel of our rental car, watching me. I put Aunt Barb's jeep in reverse and drive a few minutes down the highway to her motel. Saad stays close behind and I smile at him in the rear-view mirror, knowing full well that he can't possibly see me. Aunt Barb is close to falling asleep in the passenger seat, like I might have to carry her into her room and put her to bed like a toddler.

The Golden Eagle Motel is on the north end of Roanoke Ridge, the opposite side of town from the ranger station where Aunt Barb spent her day. It's obvious by its sign: a tacky gold eagle set against a backdrop of the American flag.

We go in as Saad waits in the car, presumably eating the rice crispy square wrapped in plastic that he bought from the diner as we were leaving. Luggage lines the walls of Aunt Barb's room; it looks like she and Professor Sorel were planning on staying awhile. Aunt Barb sits down in the wingback armchair in the corner of the room, a quilt over her legs. She blinks ever so slowly, resting her head against the wing of the chair, and calls out instructions in a voice just a touch louder than a whisper. "There's a box of chamomile tea in the cupboard to the right of the sink, dear."

I go to the small kitchenette at the back of the suite and boil a kettle on a hot plate. I pour the tea and

bring it over to Aunt Barb, setting it on the table beside her. She waves her hand over the steam before
reaching for the handle.

"Are you going to be all right, Aunt Barb?"

"I don't know what I'd do without Berton," she says.
"He's my life."

Kneeling down next to her chair, my hand on hers,
I look down at the lint and hair scattered across the
grey carpet. She lets out a long, laboured breath. She's
trying not to cry and I'm pretending not to notice the
glistening coat of saline on her eyes.

TWO

The horses reared suddenly in alarm and threw both the riders. Luckily, Roger fell off to the right and, being an experienced horseman, disengaged himself and grabbed his camera. Why? Because he had spotted what had turned their horses into mad broncos. About 100 feet ahead, on the other side of the creek bed, there was a huge, hairy creature that walked like a man!

— Ivan T. Sanderson, "First Photos of 'Bigfoot,' California's Legendary 'Abominable Snowman,'" *Argosy*, February 1968

WHEN THE LUMBER MILL CLOSED IN THE late nineties, the chamber of commerce created the Roanoke Valley Bigfoot Festival to bring business to the town a few weeks before the tourist season. There's a similar festival in Willow Creek, California, that's been around since the sixties, but since it takes place on Labor Day weekend, both festivals coexist peacefully. Roanoke Valley's festival tends to attract more Canadians, given its proximity to the border, but both festivals seem to make a pretty penny off of Bigfoot (who likely doesn't see a cent of it).

The parking lot of the Rotary Club building is full and bustles like a county fair. There's lots of denim and plaid in the crowd funnelling through the back door of the building. There are, too, a lot of Bigfoot T-shirts and Tilley hats. Saad is taken aback. This is the other side of the spectrum from what he expected.

Saad walks several steps toward the door before he realizes I'm no longer by his side. I'm fascinated by the stickers of Sasquatch prints on the backs of all the pickup trucks, every Bigfoot bumper sticker you can imagine. I want to read each one, maybe snap a few pics. They run the gamut from playful to sarcastic, some self-aware, others blindly faithful. There's one that reads *Gone Squatchin'* on a minivan, next to a pickup with a sticker that reads *Bigfoot Research Team*. One rust-covered bumper on an old Chevy has two stickers, typical bumper clichés with Sasquatch rolled in: *I Brake for Bigfoot* and *I'd rather be squatching*. I see a picture of Bigfoot with the words *Undisputed Hide and Seek Champion* that puts a smile on my face, then a faded sticker that reads *Sasquatch 2012: Anybody but Obama* and the smiles disappears. At least a dozen cars have stickers that read, simply, *I Believe*, paired with either images of Sasquatch or silhouettes of massive humanoid footprints.

"I don't get this one," Saad says, pointing to a sticker that reads *How many bear skeletons have you found out in the woods?*

"That's a reference to Grover Krantz, an anthropologist who was pro-Bigfoot. It's a counter-argument to the problem of why we don't have a Bigfoot body or any part of one. Supposedly, Krantz asked a forest ranger about the number of bear carcasses he came across in his duties, and the ranger said none. Or something like that."

As the words leave my mouth, I stop and realize how much I know about this stuff. It's like I hear my dad's voice in my head, the soundtrack to the long car rides up to the mountains. I remember the religious fervour in his voice, his thumbs drumming on the steering wheel, as he explored every theory, quoted every expert, listed the reasons he agreed or didn't.

"Is that true?" Saad asks. "About the bear carcasses?"

I shake my head. "They're rare, but they're definitely out there. I looked into this myself, read reports from Katmai National Park, which has one of the densest bear populations in the U.S. A survey of brown bear deaths near the Brooks River, in the interior, notes that only thirteen bodies had been found in thirty years. However, another study from the Pacific coast of Katmai states that seventeen carcasses had been reported in a seven-year span. The Canadian Parks Service did similar studies in four parks that surround and encompass the Rocky Mountains. Between 1990 and 2009, they only found twelve black bears that were killed by natural causes. Your average hiker or hunter probably never reports a dead bear sighting, so we have no way of knowing how many are actually out there."

Inside the Rotary Club, a disco ball hangs from the ceiling in the centre of the room. In the back corner is a small bar. The lights are off and the glass door of the fridge reveals empty shelves. The Rotary Club is obviously the social centre of the town, but nobody is planning on partying tonight.

Rows of brown folding chairs with plastic backs are set up in the middle of the room. There are only a few seats left, and a crowd lines up at the side of the room, near the table with the coffee machines on it. Old friends greet each other, introductions are made. There's an air of reunion. The faithful sit at the very front, rigidly upright like there's rebar in their spines. Saad and I stake our claim to some standing room beside the table with the coffee and the stacks of cups and bowls of creamers.

Lindsay Chiu stands behind the oak lectern at the front of the hall, double- and triple-checking the projector and her PowerPoint slides. Her dark brown hair is tied in a braid that rests on her right shoulder. The reflection of her laptop is visible in her oversized vintage-style glasses. She shifts papers around next to her computer, then looks over at a man with white hair and a white beard, dressed like a hunter on safari, who joins her at the front.

The room settles, voices drop to whispers. Every chair is now occupied by men and women who look like farmers, honest-faced people who go to church on Sunday and stop by the side of the road when a stranger is having car trouble. A line of men stand at the back of the room, arms crossed and stoic. It's a packed house. I recognize several people from cable network "documentaries" on the paranormal and cryptozoology. The Bigfoot Festival tends to draw a who's who of the squatching community.

"I want to thank you folks for coming," the bearded safari man says. "Some of you may know me from the Cryptomania website or my appearances on NatureWorld's series *Monster Hunt*. You may have even read one of my books. For those of you who don't know me, I'm Lon Colney, and I'm here tonight because, like most of you, I'm absolutely fascinated by Bigfoot."

The crowd claps. A hefty farmer-type puts four fingers to his mouth and whistles at a pitch that could shatter a champagne glass. The energy in the room is akin to that of a tent revival, and like a circuit rider in the days of old, Lon Colney is here to minister to the faithful.

"Before I introduce tonight's speaker, I just want to say a few words. As some of you may have read on Cryptomania this morning, a new species of wolf has been identified in Nepal. This species was identified from DNA taken from scat samples, which tells me two things. One, large mammals are still being identified to this very day; and two, we don't need a dead body or even a captured specimen to prove a creature's existence!"

The crowd is all-in now. Lon could ask them to stand up and join him in the hokey-pokey and it seems like they would without hesitation.

My website, Science Is Awesome, commonly called ScienceIA, posted that same story this morning, albeit with a radically different slant. *Canis lupus chanco* was thought only to be a subspecies of European grey wolf. However, when the DNA samples collected from its scat were put through GenBank, an open access database of nucleotide sequences maintained by the National Center for Biotechnology Information, they were found to represent a separate species. A new species wasn't actually discovered; the Himalayan wolf has been known to science for two centuries. Instead, an animal we already knew about was just given a new taxonomic status. But that didn't stop Lon Colney from bending the story to fit his cause.

"Think of the ape-men who hurled stones at the group of gold miners in a cabin in Ape Canyon, just up the highway from here in 1924. Or the female Sasquatch caught on tape by Roger Patterson in Bluff Creek. Or the pair of creatures filmed in this very region back in 1993. We know that something is out there. Many of us have seen it, or heard it, or found its tracks, or have even dodged its rock-throwing attacks. One day we will find the evidence, and like this Himalayan wolf, we will get the eggheads in the white lab coats to take a good, long look at what we've known all along!"

One member of the crowd shoots up out of his seat and claps furiously. There are more cheers and whistles. Saad looks at me curiously and I shrug my shoulders. Lon waves the crowd down and the noise dries up.

"Tonight we have a Ph.D. candidate from the Washington State University's Department of Anthropology. She has been on several expeditions to the jungles of Indonesia to study the behaviour of white-handed gibbons, and has come here to talk about finding Bigfoot's home range and tracking their movements using state-of-the-art computer software. Folks, put your hands together for Lindsay Chiu."

The clapping stops and Lindsay slouches in front of the microphone. Poor thing. She clears her throat and her first words are just louder than a whisper. I hate public speaking, too, it's so much easier to use a website to communicate with the world.

"Th-thank you for coming. We may as well dive right in. I've been using ecological niche modelling to predict the distribution of Sasquatches, or Bigfoot, in the Pacific Northwest, using reported sightings as my source data. Using these reports as a baseline, we were able to run them through a computer algorithm that factors in the soil type, temperature, precipitation, and tree cover and predict what ecological niche the Sasquatch finds optimal and where these conditions are most favourable. With one exception — the San Bernardino county sighting of 2010 — all the sightings occurred in matching environments."

Her shoulder shifts and the slide on the projector changes from the title screen to a map of western North America, starting with the southern tip of California and stretching up to the British Columbia–Yukon border. To the left of the map is a sketch of Bigfoot, arms swinging, looking at the audience. It's like a still frame taken from the Patterson-Gimlin film, except for one missing detail, the pendulous breasts that seem to be a constant topic of conversation in Bigfoot circles. Each sighting of Bigfoot used in the study is marked on the map as a black footprint. There is a line of these footprints starting in the Palm Springs area. It moves north in a sporadic single file until about Redding, and then expand all over northern California and up into Oregon. From there the map is covered in black footprints, clustered near the mountains but pretty busy over all the green space on the map.

"I've taken reported sightings going back as far as 1924, using filtering criteria such as the number of witnesses, physical evidence, and plausibility. Included in the data are auditory contacts with Sasquatches as well, though we've only included reports from witnesses with a lot of outdoor expertise, those who are familiar with common outdoor sounds, like those of deer, wolves, and frogs, for example. And of course, track sites have been included."

Lindsay changes the slide to one that looks identical, except that the footprints on the map are now different colours, all the colours of the rainbow.

"The colour-coding gives you the idea of when these sightings happened. As you can see, the area of highest concentration of sightings ranges from Oregon to British Columbia, and the highest concentrations of sightings in the last twenty years are in northern Washington State and B.C. The distribution of Sasquatch, according to my model, is similar to that of the American black bear, which makes sense given that the Sasquatch is, like the black bear, purportedly a large, furry, mammalian omnivore."

The slide changes to two maps side by side. The one on the left is the colourless map from the second slide. On the right is a map with a picture of a bear overlaid on the West Coast, tiny black paw prints marking its territory.

"As temperatures continue to change in the Pacific Northwest — as they have been doing steadily over the last few decades — we will likely see the remaining Sasquatch populations, as well as that of the black bear, moving to higher latitudes, and shifting farther north into British Columbia."

Standing to my right, in the back corner of the hall, is a well-coiffed man staring down at his smartphone, glancing up occasionally as if a teacher might call him out for not paying attention. He's wearing a dark, pinstripe suit with a blue shirt and tie. I can see his gold watch in the dim light. His bluetooth is still clipped to his ear. If I had to pick out the one person who doesn't belong here, it would be him.

The next slide is that of a strange-looking bear. It is large, with the long body of a polar bear, but the wide-set skull of a grizzly. Its fur is a soiled white, and there is a dark mask of hair on its face.

"This is a pizzly, sometimes called a grolar bear. It is a polar-grizzly hybrid. Incidents of this hybridization are occurring more frequently as grizzly bears migrate north in search of the cooler climate they have grown used to, and as polar bears move south in search of food as the Arctic sea ice that once provided nourishment melts away. Because of that same melting trend, bears can easily travel where there were once insurmountable mountain glaciers, and procreate with one another."

The slide changes again. Now a moose, almost completely furless, looks lost in the centre of the frame.

"Some of you have probably seen this before. It's called a ghost moose. You can see it has scratched off most of its fur as it tries to remove the ticks from its hide. This picture was taken in northwestern Alberta, Canada. The tick population has skyrocketed as the winter is no longer cold enough long enough to kill them off in great number. This is just another factor to consider. Remnant populations of Sasquatch may move farther north to avoid the increase in parasites and insect-borne diseases brought by warmer temperatures."

Saad leans over and whispers in my ear. "Is she …"

"Trolling the crowd? I think so," I say.

The slide changes again. There are three images running diagonally from the top left to the bottom right of the slide, photos of a mountaintop with years printed above them. The more recent the photo, the less snow sits on top of the mountain.

"We have seen a twenty percent decline in snowpack in the Cascade Mountains over the last century,"

Lindsay says. "Show of hands, how many of you fish the rivers and streams that run down from the mountain?"

Six or seven hands shoot up immediately, without thought or hesitation. Then the next wave of hands goes up, those of the people who took an extra second to process the question. Then there are those who are reluctant, those who feel they are being lured into a trap. Their hands rise slowly; you can see the struggle in their eyes.

"You've probably noticed the changes in fish populations in the lakes and streams here in Oregon. We see fewer chinook salmon and bull trout in these waters, as their habitat is extremely vulnerable to temperature change. Many of you are probably used to fishing the cold-water fish, salmon, for example. New species are starting to move in as the waters warm and the snow-pack shrinks with each year."

"Tell Al Gore we ain't interested," a man shouts from the back, his arms folded tightly across his body.

Lindsay continues, nervous, but persevering all the same.

"Although many theorize that Sasquatch is a vegetarian, I know many more of you suspect that its diet is very similar to that of a grizzly bear. If fish play a large part in the creature's omnivorous diet, then the radical shift in availability of fish may serve to further force the creature northward into Canada."

I watch the faces of the audience members. Lindsay's words are sinking in. These people read the articles every day about salmon die-offs, about new warm-water fish appearing both off the coast and in the rivers and streams. They have seen the local effects of a global phenomenon. Lindsay is succeeding where my site has failed: she is making climate change relevant to people whose belief systems have steered them away from the fact that man is able to tear down Creation, and can do it not with atomic bombs, but just by driving to work.

"Let's consider the amount of food a Bigfoot would require. Individual orangutans, who weigh one hundred pounds on average, eat between twenty-five hundred to eight thousand calories a day. The average black bear, weighing two hundred and forty pounds, eats around eight thousand calories a day, up to fourteen thousand as they prepare for winter. A Bigfoot, if it were to weigh four hundred pounds, would require something in the neighbourhood of six thousand calories a day. It would have to travel at least three-quarters of a mile daily to meet its dietary needs, and therefore needs a wide range to forage. Not only are large tracts of land necessary for foraging, but we must also consider uninterrupted corridors allowing individuals to breed outside of their family group, to maintain a robust and healthy population. If we consider gorillas for a second: lowland gorillas need a sixty-five-mile home range to meet their dietary needs. That's an area greater than the town of Bend. Bigfoot will likely require a lot of real estate to survive. Although much of the Pacific Northwest is an unbroken swath of wilderness, human development, habitat loss, and forest fires will prove detrimental to healthy Bigfoot populations."

The audience is pensive again. People lean back in the seats, stroke their chins, furrow their eyebrows. They've been taken off the subject of climate change and are back on Bigfoot. Lindsay herself doesn't have much in the way of a natural charisma, which is why science communicators have to work so hard against the slick, polished PR professionals who make their millions sewing doubt about the dangers of tobacco or fossil fuels.

"According to the Forest Service, wildfire season is growing in both duration and area affected," Lindsay says. "With these other stressors, and the habitat loss that comes with expanding human populations, it seems safe to assert that the remaining Sasquatch populations will migrate north to the cooler, less populated interior of British Columbia. Now, if you're of the mind that you'd rather have a corpse to prove the existence of Bigfoot, fire and starvation may increase the odds of finding one. All we can be certain of is that this region is changing, and the animals who like it the way it's been for millennia will have to flee to the north."

The applause starts slowly, softly. An older lady with a mess of curls, a cross around her neck dangling over the lip of her turtleneck, starts clapping furiously. She, out of sympathy perhaps, is cheerleading the crowd. Many don't want to clap, but either rural hospitality or the herd mentality kicks in.

●　●　●

Since I've been standing this whole time, I'm the first one to the table with complimentary coffee. As I pour, I see Rick Driver, the notorious hoaxer, in my peripheral vision. Wearing a baseball cap and denim shirt, he approaches me from across the room, chewing on his lower lip and hooking his thumbs in his belt. He tilts his head back to look down his nose at me. I pretend that stirring a Styrofoam cup filled with black coffee requires a lot of attention.

"I know you," he says.

"Pardon me?"

"I know you," he says again. "You're Nate Reagan's girl."

His words catch me off guard.

"You knew my dad?"

"Oh sure, me and Nate were thick as thieves."

It's hard to picture my dad collaborating with a man who looks like he models his appearance after Larry the Cable Guy. He smiles at me like I'm edible and he's starving. I take a small step back and feel the table press against the back of my legs.

"You were just a tot last time I saw you," he says. "Now look at you, all grown up."

"I don't remember you," I say.

"No reason why you should. Like I said, you were just a tot," he says, looking back toward the front of the room. "A lotta people got sucked into this. They came here in good faith to talk about a subject close to their hearts."

"That's a lot of sentimentality for a hoaxer extraordinaire."

"That's the game," he says, then he points to the projector, which has left a square of blue on the screen. "Not this. If she wasn't such a tasty —"

"Laura," Saad calls out to me.

He is standing next to a bookish, sandy-haired man in his late thirties to early forties, who is wearing a wool sweater a little too thick for the spring climate. He sticks out in this room, looking more like he belongs among ivy-covered bricks on a campus somewhere.

"This is Duncan Laidlaw," Saad says.

"Excuse me," I say without looking at Rick Driver.

"I thought you might appreciate a rescue," Saad whispers, when I get to him.

"You have no idea," I say through clenched teeth, smiling at Duncan. "So you're Duncan Laidlaw," I say, shaking hands gently with the academic-looking man.

"Indeed," he says in his thick English accent. "Everyone here seems to expect something different when they meet me. I think it's my name. I sound like a police detective or action hero or something."

"I was picturing Alan Grant from *Jurassic Park*," I say.

"Oh, well, sorry to disappoint," he says.

"Not at all," I say.

"I'm delighted to meet you," he says. "I'm a huge fan of your website. I was just saying to Saad that your website stops me from making one of my own. I would have loved to capitalize on the millennial love of science, but I've missed the boat, I'm afraid. You're doing such a smashing job I figure there's no point in trying, so I'm left to my little blog."

"That's very kind of you to say. I'm actually a huge fan of your blog. And your papers have generated a ton of content for my site, especially your work on plesiosaurs."

"You're the one who is very kind. Are you here to cover this circus for your site?"

"I'm here on personal business, actually, but instead of sitting around my motel waiting for daylight, I thought this would be an interesting talk."

"It certainly was, in more ways than one. The use of niche modelling is novel. Speaking of, can you explain to me why Americans say *nitch* instead of *niche*, as though it's a place where cars that swerve off the road end up?"

"We have to pick and choose which French words we pronounce correctly. Sounding American is very important to us."

"Undoubtedly."

"I assume, Duncan, that you dismiss Bigfoot as nonsense?"

"That's a complex question for me," he says. "Oh, don't look so surprised. I didn't come here to point fingers and mock."

"I'm sorry," I say.

"I certainly won't dismiss the idea outright. It doesn't seem scientific to rule out a possibility with little or no investigation, and I do believe that the idea of Sasquatch has a prior plausibility. We're not talking about a massive marine reptile that has been extinct for sixty-five million years surfacing in a Scottish loch that only came about after the last ice age."

Lindsay Chiu falls into orbit around us, shifting her weight side to side like a metronome. Her chin is tilted down at her collarbone and she looks up at Duncan. I think of a reason to include her in the conversation — I've been her enough times at enough conferences.

"Excellent presentation," Duncan says, before I get a chance to say anything.

"Thank you," she says. "And thank you for coming."

"It was a pleasure," he says. "Have you met Laura Reagan?"

"How do you do?" Lindsay says, rather formally.

"Laura is the founder of Science Is Awesome," Duncan says. "And her name also starts with the letter *L*, so you have that in common. We're not quite in *Superman* comics, though, are we?"

We both look at him.

"Like Lex Luthor and Lois Lane," Lindsay says, finally.

"Precisely," Duncan says. "I'd hoped I wasn't the only comic book nerd here, as is so often the case."

"On the subject of superheroes: Lindsay, do you spend a lot of time trying to secretly slip climate change and conservation science into cryptozoological lectures?" I ask.

"It's my personal crusade," she says. "My obsession. Sometimes that means a little live-trolling."

"Science communication can be an uphill battle," I say.

"Love is a battlefield," Lindsay says, smiling.

"Pat Benatar," Saad says, proving that he's still awake.

"Some of us have to do it," she says. "There's so much terrible science journalism out there."

"I'd like to think I do my part," I say.

"We all have parts to play before the world boils over," she says. "Or freezes over, if that's your point of view."

Ouch.

I know exactly what she's talking about. Last year, I ran a story on my site based off of a press release from the National Astronomy Meeting. A team of scientists were predicting, based on mathematical modelling, that we may experience a decline in solar activity, known as a Maunder minimum. This phenomenon is thought to have caused the "Little Ice Age" in the seventeenth century. I ran the story with a headline claiming we were approaching another ice age. Worse still, I posted an image beneath the headline of a man with his fur collar up, a wool hat pulled down to his eyebrows and a comically confused expression on his face. I knew the story was sensational, but I wanted to generate traffic to the site and interest in factors affecting climate. A story like that, of rapid climate change, gets picked up by mainstream media. And mine did. The *Telegraph* in the U.K. ran the story on their front page. Comment pages, the natural habitat of climate-denying trolls, were awash in discussions of the validity of mathematical modelling as it pertains to climate change, something they usually argue against.

Was my headline hasty? Yes. Did it succeed in generating interest in the site and in the science be-hind climate change? Certainly. Had I become the sensationalist media who encourages the distortion of fact in favour of attention? I'm afraid so.

Within days I was torn apart. Doubtful News and other skeptical sites highlighted the poor coverage of the story. I personally wrote three follow-ups accepting blame, one of which featured an interview with the head researcher responsible for the original press release. I ran special pieces written by several important science communication experts about the failure of the media, my own included.

What struck me the most after the dust settled was that my readership was up. It wasn't a huge leap in page views, I can't even be sure it wasn't a natural fluctuation given the steady increase prior to the story, but it was up. All in all, the controversy made little difference — and that's what hurt. Despite the popularity of my site, the interviews I'd given, the puff pieces written about my success, my audience still didn't expect perfection. They didn't hold me in the high regard that I thought they would. Nobody was outraged by my lapse in journalistic standards, because they hadn't expected them in the first place.

But the true believers, the science faithfuls, those who live by the peer-review process, the Lindsay Chius of the world, they'll never let it go. They will always remind me that I'm not one of them, that the letters *B.Sc.* are all that follow my name on my business card.

"The only difference between a wise man and a fool," I say, "is a wise man learns from his mistakes."

"I don't think that's the saying," Lindsay says.

"I think it's close enough," Duncan says, making an attempt at diplomacy. "I'm told there's a pub down the road where some of this lot will be grabbing a pint later, would you two care to join?"

"Ordinarily I'd jump at the chance to pick your brain and eat fries out of a paper-lined basket, but tomorrow is a big day," I say.

"Understood," Duncan says. "Raincheck on the brain-picking."

"I'd love to," Lindsay says.

The crowd dissipates like dust on a country highway. Saad and I wait a little. Saad loves crowds, he navigates them well. He can see a crowd as people, rather than just an undulating wall constantly becoming tighter and tighter.

Rick Driver catches up with us and says, "Girl, if you think I'm a fraud, that limey fella will knock your socks off." He walks away through the dark parking lot toward a big red pickup.

"I don't care," I call after him. "I'm not here for Bigfoot."

"You're here to find that professor fella," he calls back from beside his truck. "Do you know how many people go missing in national parks every year? Do you? And they never find 'em."

THREE

A number of gentlemen from Lytton and points east of that place who, after considerable trouble and perilous climbing, succeeded in capturing a creature which may truly be called half man and half beast. "Jacko," as the creature has been called by his capturers, is something of the gorilla type …

— *Daily Colonist*, July 4, 1884

I LIE AWAKE, LISTENING TO EIGHTEEN-wheelers thunder down the highway outside my window. I try not to think about Professor Sorel, alone in the woods, possibly injured, shivering as night takes hold. Forcing my eyes shut, I try to think about something else, anything else. What pops into my head is the offer to buy Science Is Awesome — it'll take my lawyer some time to pore over the paperwork the tech giant

Geocomm sent over after the video call three days ago. And then guilt, for even considering selling off something I worked so hard to build. I never planned on this life, I'm not sure it's the right fit. And who wouldn't want to be set for life?

I change tracks again. Rick Driver's playing in my head now. What did he mean, about being *thick as thieves* with Dad? And that nonsense about Duncan Laidlaw?

From the other bed, mattress springs creak as Saad turns over from one side to the other. His comforter is pulled up high over his head like a cocoon.

I lift my own blanket up and slip out of bed, curling my toes on the carpet. I sit on the floor and lean against the wall, balancing my laptop on my knees, the monitor pointed away from Saad. I try not to disturb him with the glare from the screen and am conscious of the sound of typing and mouse clicks.

My browser is up and my email is open. The Geocomm offer is now halfway down my inbox. I open a new tab and try to push it out of my mind.

Entering Rick Driver's name into the search bar reveals how much of a circus the world of cryptozoology can be. The photos that come up of Driver show him wearing hats which are plugging websites, supplement lines, local hardware stores, and so on. Then of course there are the headlines: *Texas Man Claims He Shot Bigfoot. Local Man Has Bigfoot Body On Ice. Dead Bigfoot On Display in Lubbock.* The dates of these stories span a decade, and in each one, Driver claims to have come by the body of a Bigfoot by some new means: nailing steaks to trees and shooting the creature. Accidentally hitting one with his truck. Finding one poisoned after it raided his campsite and ate all his chewing tobacco. All in all, it is estimated that he's made half a million dollars touring his supposed Sasquatch corpses around rural America.

When his first fraud was exposed, Driver claimed that a mysterious alphabet agency came in black vehicles and took his Bigfoot corpse. Since he already spread the word of his possession of the body, he felt compelled to deliver on his word. He was so compelled he took an ape costume and stuffed it with roadkill. The second time, he claimed that he was the victim of a hoax. The third time, his defence was simply *can't you people take a joke?*

If cop dramas have taught me anything, it's that serial offenders always start small, before escalating to things like killing. Perhaps Rick Driver had to take a few dry runs before becoming a half-a-million-dollar hoaxer.

I start digging a little deeper. Several online profiles depict him as a *professional Bigfoot hunter*, but there's very little about him before his first hoax. There is one thread in a chat room about Driver serving in the military, but there are no citations and no further corroborating data points.

I decide to take him out of the equation and instead search only for Bigfoot hoaxes in the Texas area, dating back two decades. There is surprisingly little to find, even if you switch to regional nomenclature such as *skunk ape*, *stink ape*, or *swamp ape*. Rick Driver is pretty much the father of Bigfoot hoaxing in that part of the country, and the only hoaxes on record are his masterpieces — no practice sketches.

Thing about Rick Driver is, yes, he comes off as the prototypical Texan — but what if that's part of the con? Even the most well-educated U.S. president uses terms like *folks*, and injects some down-home twang when stumping among the rural working class. What if Driver's good old boy accent and manner were just schtick? It occurs to me that he might have travelled northwestward — to study with the masters, so to speak. When trying a con, it's probably best to start out on those conditioned to believe. You don't try a Christian faith-healing racket on a bunch of atheists at a skeptic's convention.

I start digging through all the banner cases, the blockbusters of the Bigfoot world: the PG film, the Jerry Crew casts, even my father's own footage. One incident sticks out, for its originality. In the late eighties, a trio of men staged a Sasquatch sighting along Highway 20 near Winthrop in northern Washington. A Bigfoot appeared at the side of the highway, just as a coach bus crossed the bridge over Early Winters Creek. Twenty people saw the ape-man disappear into the woods. Word spread like wildfire.

The genius of that hoax was the lack of video to be analyzed. In fact, this story could have played a major part in the Bigfoot canon — but for the fact that it was too perfect. Whenever a hoax is that perfect, somebody will want credit, and eventually two out of three of the men came forward. One of the men was on the bus during the sighting — in fact, he was the first passenger to spot the beast as it emerged from a rocky outcropping and wove between yellow cedars. The second man had made the suit, complete with large rubber feet designed to leave oversized tracks in the soil. A third man, who chose to remain anonymous, wore the suit. It doesn't appear that they made any money out of the hoax; it was more of a test just to see if they could do it.

In the photo accompanying the article are the two men, made of halftone dots on a base of blue. They share atavistic traits with hipsters, the lumberjack look with overstylized facial hair. They look like one half of Creedence Clearwater Revival. The one on the left is the suit maker, Donald Oreskes. The thinner, shaggier one on his right looks familiar. The caption beneath identifies him as Oregon native John Driver Junior.

Sometime between 1990 and 2004, Donald Oreskes left the picture, and John became *Rick*.

The fascinating takeaway from the Winthrop hoax is what the eyewitness accounts described. The bus passengers — those not in cahoots with the hoaxers — had described the creature they saw as over seven feet tall. But when Oreskes and Driver produced the suit, which was a modified gorilla costume, it was designed to fit a man no taller than six foot one. Given the region and its history, it seems the witnesses saw what they expected to see; with no sense of scale, the creature they saw was stretched by their imaginations.

I search for a Donald Oreskes in Washington, and it looks like he might own a bookstore on the outskirts of Kennewick. There's a phone number for the store and I contemplate calling it in the morning.

Finally, before I go back to bed, I type my father's name plus *John Driver Junior* into the search engine. If Rick had seen me when I was little — before I was *all grown up* — he was probably still going by the name John Jr.

I'm relieved when I get zero results.

FOUR

Most accounts tell of giant boulders being hurled against the cabin, and say some even fell through the roof, but this was not the case. There were very few large rocks around in that area. It is true that many smaller ones were hurled at the cabin, but they did not break through the roof, but hit with a bang, and rolled off.

— Fred Beck, *I Fought the Ape-Men of Mount St. Helens, WA*, September 27, 1967

HIGHWAY 49 SNAKES THROUGH PINE TREES and mountains before becoming the main street of Roanoke Valley. The sun climbs slowly over the peaks of the trees. There's no wasting daylight at a time like this. Aunt Barb looks alert in the rear-view mirror. She's quiet and I doubt there's anything I could say to assuage her worries. Aside from "good morning," she hasn't said a word since we picked her up. Saad slows down as a man with a stop sign, wearing a hard hat and orange vest, stands in the middle of the road. Workmen in a cherry picker are hanging a banner that stretches across the two-lane highway. *Bigfoot Welcomes You!* the sign reads as the workmen hoist it taught, high above the asphalt. Shops appear with silhouettes of Bigfoot in the windows. Advertisements for Bigfoot burgers, Bigfoot shakes, Bigfoot fries, Bigfoot hats, Bigfoot everything are visible from the street. The smell of fresh pancakes wafts over from the diner on the corner. The banner above their door reads *Bigfoot Breakfast Special $3.99 All Weekend Long.*

A camera crew is in the centre of town, shooting establishing footage for *The Million Dollar Bigfoot Hunt.* The white-and-green NatureWorld van is parked by the curb, its back doors open. A cameraman pans across the sidewalk to capture the scene, the mood, the worship of all things Bigfoot.

The road curves and dips down deeper in the valley part of Roanoke Valley. We cross a bridge that runs overtop of the Klamath River. Half a mile farther up, one of the mountain streams merges with the Klamath, adding to it the clean, clear water pouring down from ice packs high in the Cascade Mountains. The Klamath itself starts in the plains to the east and cuts a path through the mountains in defiance of every other waterway in the region. *National Geographic* called the Klamath "a river upside down" due to its odd geography.

On the bank of the river, on my side of the car, a hulking dark wood structure looms menacingly back from the road. It's an old sawmill, the water wheel long removed and boards along the side fallen off. A smaller, newer structure sits in front, closer to the road; its sign reads *Bigfoot Museum and Art Gallery.*

The road winds around a bend and then there's nothing but trees growing straight up on radical inclines, one mountain rising above all the others. It sits dominantly, the silverback of the group, wearing a crown of clouds. It's easy to forget that we just left town. There is only the one road, the one scar on the land as evidence of a human presence, until we reach the turn-off for the ranger station.

A command centre, set up at the ranger station at the end of the road, points toward the mountains. A dozen cars are parked on the gravel shoulders on either side of the road, most of them with insignia on their doors. I make note of the coats of arms of the county sheriff, the Park Service, the Department of the Interior, and a white pickup that just says *Roanoke County.* An army of volunteers awaits their directions. Some are squatchers that I recognize from Lindsay Chiu's talk last night, others are from a citizen science organization I've met before called Oregon Budwatchers. They record the exact date and time when buds open in the spring, allowing scientists to gauge the effects of climate change, among other things, on these forests.

The ranger station is an army-green single-storey building, set back from the road by a well-manicured lawn, with a flagpole out front, a plaque at its base. It was built in the thirties, among the thousands of projects created by FDR under the National Industrial Recovery Act of 1933. It looks like a summer camp, not a federal building, but there's a tension, an urgency in the people coming in and out, descending the three stone steps and heading out into the parking lot.

I stay a half step behind Aunt Barb while Saad trails behind us. Two black birds fly overhead; their silhouettes against the red-purple sky look like those of waterfowl, but I can't be sure. There's a crowd outside the ranger station. A silver-haired superintendent stands at the front, pointing clusters of people to different trails. We approach as the search parties split up. He spots Aunt Barb and walks toward us. One younger ranger, a man with a tawny beard and sharp blue eyes, also joins us and stands at attention like a soldier.

"Good morning, ma'am," the superintendent says, taking his hat off to reveal his widow's peak.

"Hello," Aunt Barb says. "This is …"

She points toward me but her words fail.

"I'm Laura Reagan, this is my friend, Saad Javed."

"Thank you for coming. I'm told you have some insight into where Professor Sorel may have been hiking."

"He told Aunt Barb that he was going to a spot my father filmed back in the nineties. My dad never drew a map or anything, but he brought me there enough times that I think I can find it by memory."

"We sent out three teams in that general area yesterday, but they came up empty."

"Perhaps we will have better luck," I say.

"Do you have any prior SAR experience?" the superintendent asks, his tone too flat for me to decipher any implications.

"No, sir," I say. "I have hiked these mountains since I was six years old, I've taken part in several field expeditions tracking different forms of wildlife, mainly weasels and muskrats. I have first aid and lifeguard training and I run at least two marathons a year. I figure I'm good enough to sidekick one of your rangers."

"What about your friend there?" he says, pointing to Saad.

"Well," I say, looking at Saad. Even his sighs cry out bookworm. "He's an experienced hiker and rock climber, with several degrees."

The superintendent turns and waves the younger ranger closer. The tawny-bearded man — who hasn't moved a muscle the entire time we've been here, just studied us coldly with his ice-blue eyes — sidles up next to his boss and looks us both over, those eyes shooting from me to Saad and back. He holds his head still the whole time. He reminds me of Joshua Jackson, but more handsome, less baby-faced.

"This is Ted Cassavetes, he'll be escorting you up the mountain with Moira Hearn, a paramedic." The superintendent tugs on his sleeve to get a better look at the face of his watch. "She'll be joining us shortly."

Ranger Cassavetes gives a little half bow to me and nods at Saad. He holds his hands behind his back, sticking his chest out. The name Ted doesn't seem to fit a man in his early thirties, and a Greek surname like Cassavetes seems at odds with his blue eyes and light features. He's athletic looking without being muscle-bound, and he looks sure of himself.

"How much SAR experience does Ranger Cassavetes have, if you don't mind my asking?" You've got to be ready to jump right into the jargon when you write or blog about science. I can see it's no different here. I doubt either of these men have said *search and rescue* out loud for years.

"He's the best on my staff. He's even done aerial and sea SAR when he was in the navy," the superintendent says.

A minute later, we stand in front of Ranger Ted's truck. Laid out on the hood is a map of green blotches, with blue cracks for each river and wrinkles to signify the topography. Ted draws two fingers in a circle around Roanoke Ridge.

"No emergency beacon, no GPS, not even a cellphone," Ted says. "It's like your professor wanted to get lost."

"How about a little compassion? We can worry about blaming the victim later," I say.

Ranger Ted raises his eyebrows and opens his hands at me like I've just pulled a gun on him.

"Still, a man his age has no business up here alone."

"Professor Sorel's been hiking around these mountains since before you were born."

"Like Ali versus Holmes."

"What?"

"They're boxers —"

"I know who they are, I don't see the parallel," I say.

"Meaning no matter how good you were, you have to know when to quit." He checks his watch, gazes off at the mountains beyond the trees.

Moira the paramedic finally arrives with a small backpack and a medical kit slung over her shoulder. She nods at Ranger Ted and makes a quick introduction to Saad and I. Before we finish introductions, Ted is already inside his truck and turning the engine. Saad and I squeeze into the back of Ted's truck, he and Moira sit in the front.

A ghostly mist rises through the forest canopy and a woodpecker's call echoes between the trees. We start out from the ranger station with the sun at our backs and the mountain before us. Ted drives up a steep and bumpy dirt road once used by miners to access their claims scattered over the eastern face of the mountain. There's been something of a clampdown on mining in this area by the Bureau of Land Management after a slew of new by-laws and the enforcement of those by-laws. There have been small protests covered by local news, but limited coverage nationally speaking. I only know about it because I always pay a special bit of attention to this area.

The landscape has changed in the years since my last visit. We drive along a dirt road taking us north-west and soon it's like there was no ranger station, no paved road, nothing but wilderness. The beauty, of the trees beginning to bloom, the stream that runs alongside the road we're on, the mountain peaks in the distance — it makes it easy to see why people believe in God. It's hard to believe such perfection could happen by accident. Looking down into the stream, the cold, fresh water flowing from high in the mountain, I see purity. I see it as my father would, prime cold-water fishing, like a vein on the surface of the earth just waiting for someone to come along and scoop up a bull trout. A month from now the spring chinook fishery will open and this whole area will be overrun by a bait-and-tackle army.

"Do you get a lot of folks coming through here looking for Sasquatch?" I ask, leaning forward, holding the back of Ted's seat.

"We get our share," he says. "They burst in here loud and proud, with patches on their jackets and stickers on their gear that say *Bigfoot Hunters' Squad*, *Operation Sasquatch Search*, or *Northwest Cryptozoological Society*. Then you get the undercovers."

"The undercovers?"

"The people who try to act like regular outdoorsmen, hikers or fisherman or what have you. But then they start to pal up to you, start asking questions like 'seen anything strange out here?' Or my favourite, 'how many bear skeletons have you come across?' Listen, if there's something like a Bigfoot out here, I'd have heard it by now, or seen its tracks," Ted says.

Saad, who has been staring out the window at the beauty passing him by, chuckles and turns toward me. I meet him with a smile. He started this trip as a Bigfoot novice, but I have a feeling he'll be a full-blown expert by the time we're through.

"What gets me," Ted says, "is the number of people who visit here for the wilderness, the hiking trails and wildlife, and who see Sasquatch as a fringe benefit. They don't come here to see the beast, but they accept that he exists and would consider it a huge bonus if they saw him. Like seeing a grizzly bear or something."

"So he's become tacitly accepted," I say as we hit a bump on the road.

"I think the more people live in cities, their eyes glued to screens, the less they know about what actually exists. The woods become a mystery, and since ninety-nine percent of the population don't come out here and see the deer and the bears and the wolves, Bigfoot or Sasquatch becomes just as possible to them."

"There are wolves out here?" Saad asks, a tremor in his voice.

Ted winks into the rear-view mirror. "You bet. According to the latest wolf report, the state's wolf population has increased by thirty-six percent in the last year. That makes one hundred and ten individuals. Isn't that great?"

All of a sudden, the road stops. The parallel tire ruts come to an end and there's nothing but a wall of trees ahead of us. We get out and slam the truck doors shut in rhythm, and the woods go silent. It takes a few seconds for nature's symphony to begin anew. Backpack straps are securely fastened, clicked into place. Ted's GPS unit is clipped to the left strap of his pack. He radios the station to report our exact location and time of arrival.

Growing out of the tire ruts is a footpath leading up into the mountains. As we follow the path, branches hosting the first buds of spring brush against us. Lindsay Chiu's words swim through my head, circling like sharks. She was right. The winters in western North America just aren't as cold as they used to be, and each branch that wipes across my arms or thighs may carry a tick just waiting to latch on and give me Lyme disease.

When the trees have cleared enough and I can see the summit of the mountain, I remember the one thing about this place — more than ticks, more than any animal — that sends a shiver down my spine. Acrophobia would be fine; fearing heights makes sense and falling down a mountain is a real threat to hikers. Volcanophobia, on the other hand — my rational brain can't fathom it, yet here it is. The childish fear, from when Dad would tell me about all the active volcanoes here in Oregon and up in Washington. The scariest to me was Three Fingered Jack; it sounded less like a geographical feature and more like a disfigured serial killer stalking teen lovers in parked cars. Mom tried to assure me that I had nothing to worry about, and I know she was right, but the TV news couldn't help themselves, running footage of the 1980 eruption of Mount St. Helens every time there was a minor eruption somewhere in the Cascade Range.

The trees grow thick again and I can't see the mountain anymore. Ted keeps his head down as branches reach out over the trail and take swipes at him. A strange sound fills the trees ahead, impossible to pinpoint. It starts out as a low *chuck-chuck-chuck* sound, rising into a *chukar-chukar-chukar* before becoming a loud and intense *chuckara-chuckara-chuckara*.

"What's that?" I ask.

"Sssshhh, it's Bigfoot," Ted says.

"Funny."

"It's a type of partridge called a chukar, for obvious reasons," Ted says.

"I don't remember ever hearing that, and I used to camp here a lot."

"They usually stay in drier areas to the east, but I've noticed there are a few around here. With the drought conditions we've had the last few years, the chukar is finding itself more and more at home."

We take a few steps forward. I repeat the name *chukar* in my head so I won't forget it. The brush is still dry and crunches underfoot.

"There!" Ted says, jabbing his finger out like he's drawing a gun.

An oddly handsome bird, smaller than a chicken, with a cinnamon-coloured back and red eyes with a black mask over them, runs out of the tall grass.

"They're originally from India. Released in Oregon in 1951 for hunting purposes," Ted says as we keep moving higher and higher up the mountainous terrain.

I will never tell him, but Ted is pretty impressive. He spotted the chukar without slowing down and scanning the area with binoculars; he just knows where to look, and he doesn't let it interfere with his primary objective. He keeps moving up the mountain, not forgetting that we have a mission. Even his facts are delivered as an afterthought, words just to fill the space as we continue what we set out to do. He has adapted perfectly to his environment.

"There's nowhere else like this on Earth," Ted says. "This is where the Cascade, Klamath, and Siskiyou mountain ranges meet. Three unique ecosystems colliding with each other."

The elevation gain on the mountain is gradual and scaling it requires no special skills and no mountaineering experience. Those who expect the Sasquatch to be a specially adapted superclimber would never look here. The relative ease of hiking this mountain should make it a popular destination, but it doesn't seem to attract the same number of tourists as the Three Sisters or Broken Top. That's likely due to its isolation and distance from growing urban centres like Bend and the resort community of Sunriver.

Tree roots exposed by erosion form a tricky latticework, snares like trappers have used all over these parts for over a century. Ted slows down. We all slow down, stop scanning for traces of Professor Sorel in order to place each footstep carefully. Between certain roots are little burrows. The path we follow now is more a game trail than a human one. Ted's quadriceps bulge in his khaki park ranger pants as he takes the hill.

Ted stops in his tracks and points to the sky. I stop on a dime and Saad crashes into my backpack. Ted kneels down and I peek over his shoulder to get a look at what has captured his attention. He looks back at me.

"A boot print," he says. "Fresh."

The track is crisp, clear, like the person who made it wanted us to see the brand name on the arch. It was definitely made after the rain that fell yesterday evening.

"Could it be the professor's?" I ask.

"Not too many other people have a reason to be out this way, but I can't prove it."

Dad taught me to look for intent in tracks. His first lesson was a set of coyote tracks. He asked me if I could tell the difference between coyote tracks and dog tracks. Candice, our black lab, was a still a pup then, about the size of a coyote, and she lived outside, so her claws were not blunt like those of most dogs. I couldn't see a difference — I tried to notice features in the mud that differed from the prints our own dog made, but there was nothing. Dad said the difference was intent. Dogs are constantly having fun, sniffing every tree, looping around. Coyotes either want to eat or return to their den, that's all. When you know how an animal moves and why, you can predict where it will move to.

. • .

I know Professor Sorel will be carrying the same survival kit I am. Old-time woodsmen like Professor Sorel and my father always tout their virtues. A good survival kit can be packed inside a tobacco tin and fit comfortably in your pocket. Dad's looked effortless, as though they were run-of-the-mill, everyday accessories. Living in Cleveland, I don't have much need for waterproof matches, flints, candles, fish hooks and line, a compass, snare wire, a flexible saw, or a beta light. Luckily, you can't drive around the Pacific Northwest without finding plenty of camping-supply stores dotting the highway side. The survival kit shopping list is written in permanent marker on one of the fatty folds of my brain. I do have a magnifying glass at home, and a needle and thread, as well as the old tobacco tin my dad gave me when we made my first survival kit together. I also assembled a rudimentary medical kit with bandages, analgesics, antihistamines, antibiotics, water-sterilizing tablets, and potassium permanganate. I threw in a condom for good measure — a common tactic among soldiers, as they make great expandable water bags.

I have this one memory of my dad before he went off to war. We were in a park, having a picnic, when my mom suddenly shrieked. A big green praying mantis had crawled onto our blanket. Dad reached around behind the critter and plucked it from the blanket, setting it gently down in his palm. He held the insect out to me, not close enough to be really scary, but enough that it felt like bugs were crawling on my skin.

The world is full of wonders, little darling, we gotta appreciate them, he said.

There's no telling how much of that memory is the truth. Memory is not reliable, there are plenty of studies to back that up. Details get dropped, some added, years and emotions act as editors. I'd like to have known more about the man Dad was before he shipped out to the Persian Gulf to fight in a war, the reasons for which are largely forgotten. When I see photos of him from that time, I realize how truly young he was when he became a husband, a father, and a soldier. He was four years younger than I am now when he went to Iraq.

The war must have changed him — it's hard to imagine that such a thing hadn't — but I can't be sure. Mom assumed that when Dad came out of the army it would only be a matter of time before he worked a nine-to-five and settled into a routine. Instead, Dad worked odd jobs while Mom was a receptionist at a nearby elementary school. He never took on commitments that required him to go to a particular jobsite for more than two days in a row. If he weren't so skilled a man, this may have gone unnoticed. But people around town liked Dad, they loved his work, and he was seen as fundamentally honest, like he'd never rip you off. If anything he charged too little to fix an eavestrough or repair a set of broken stairs.

Still, the days after he got back were some of the happiest of my life. We went camping in the mountains almost every weekend. Sometimes, during the week, when I was in school, Dad would go up to the mountains and fish or hunt, sometimes he'd camp overnight. I loved the father-daughter time, and I learned to love the outdoors. Mom stayed home. As I child, I thought nothing of it. *Mom's not much of a camper*, Dad told me. That seemed reasonable. I didn't like art class or soccer, and if I'd had the option to stay home from them I would have.

The first time I said *no* to a father-daughter camping trip, Dad looked at me as though I were a stranger on the street asking him for money. That one look still haunts me: I see it when I think of him and I almost feel ill. I was twelve, I had gotten my first period and I couldn't tell him. I cried in a stall in the washroom at school, knowing he'd be annoyed with me, but I was too embarrassed to tell him why I didn't feel up to going. How do you explain that to a man who never once saw you as a girl?

It took me years to see that Dad needed these trips more than I did. He needed the peace of the forests, the numbing cold of mountain streams. He even grew to need Bigfoot.

In the trail in front of us, a branch, jeweled with the opening buds of spring, has been snapped. Its tip points downward toward the earth. Ted pauses at this, looks back at me and nods. A rock the size of a softball lies in the middle of the trail, muddy side up. Another sign of recent disturbance. There are no pockmarks in the soil, no gaping hole left missing a rock. There's no reason, as far as I can tell, to carry a rock and drop it right there in the middle of the trail.

As the hill becomes steeper we see that the tracks change. More weight is shifted to the ball of the foot. The impressions look as though they were left by a horse's hooves. There are more rocks on either side of the trail and the footprints are spaced farther apart and weave side to side, almost in a zigzag pattern. Ted walks ahead, faster, impetuously.

To the right of the trail is a tree stump about my height. It is long dead, barkless and bleached in the sun, like a big femur jutting from the dirt. The stump is riddled with holes, one the circumference of a human face, but the largest is at the base, a burrow fit for a raccoon with trails of mulch fanning out from it. In the middle of the rust-coloured mulch sits a rock, similar to the one earlier on the trail. There's a dent halfway up the stump that looks recent.

"We got someone over here!" Ted calls out.

He moves left and I, after a quick glance over to Moira and Saad, move right. Before me, the hillside folds inward into a valley that runs halfway down the incline before flattening out like a dustpan.

The first thing I see are hiking boots pointing toward the summit. Then the rest of the body, arms spread like Christ on the cross.

The body isn't Professor Sorel's. It's Rick Driver's.

I catch myself thinking *Thank God*, which is ethically and philosophically complicated for me. But I can't help but be relieved. Ted holds an arm out toward me as if to ward me off, like I might touch the corpse or attempt CPR on it. Any second now I expect the body to convulse and laugh, pointing fingers at us, and say, *Boy, you should have seen the look on your face.* But the body doesn't move.

There's a gash in his forehead, blood crusting around the edges. Otherwise he's fresh, untouched by scavengers, and his skin still has some colour to it. His back is arched because of the backpack under the torso, and his plaid shirt is open, revealing a T-shirt with the words *Moustache Rides Are Free* written beneath a cartoon handlebar moustache very similar to his own. His eyes are wide and stare up at a gap in the forest canopy. The sky is a beautiful, clear blue, and if there is a heaven it looks like the door is open.

Several feet down the incline is his cap, upside down on a bed of moss. A few feet farther off is a rock, the top half of which is covered in dirt. There is a small crater and trail in the reddish soil where it landed and rolled. I'm reminded of the first post I put up on my site about the sailing stones of Death Valley. Around where I'm standing, I can see three, four, five more stones just like it, tossed down from some place higher on the incline.

Moira comes over the ridge and Saad follows behind. Ted takes his GPS from his backpack's strap and starts pressing buttons. He unzips his jacket, reaches in and plucks the radio that dangles over his clavicle and calls the ranger station. He's careful not to use the victim's name over the radio, as is protocol. After being told to "sit tight," he surveys the area quickly and takes a deep breath.

"We lose a dozen people to falls every year," Ted says without specifying who *we* is.

"Look at those rocks," I say.

"Yeah?"

"You see a lot of rocks go flying off a mountaintop under their own power? Somebody threw those, they didn't just happen to fall like that," I say.

"It's not so hard to believe," he says. "Rock slides happen."

"You think someone did this on purpose?" Saad asks.

"I … I can't be sure. But look at how and where the rocks landed. It's a very small area, like he was targeted. If this was a rock slide, we should see more craters, more trails, evidence that the rocks rolled down the hill."

"Not necessarily," Ted chimes in.

"Why would somebody want to kill him?" Saad asks.

I kneel down near the body and point to his T-shirt.

"Could be a business rival," I say. "Driver was pricing the competition out of business."

"How about a little compassion?" Ted says, his tone high enough to be mocking.

"Don't get too close," Moira says. "We don't want to disturb the scene."

"Yeah, good call," Ted says. "Laura, you and Saad stay back, please." Without taking his eyes off the body, he waves us back the way we came. "We'll have to get a SAIT crew up here," he says to Moira.

"What about them?" Moira asks, pointing a thumb in our direction.

"The last thing I need is for something to happen to them. I'll get them back to the station once the SAIT crew arrives and the scene has been secured."

Saad and I walk toward a log that is buttressed on the incline between two trees. The log is hollow and looks as though it's been home to many different creatures. There's scat on the end of the log; where it touches the wood, it spreads outward like the end of an exploding cartoon cigar.

"A mustelid, something from the weasel family," I say, pointing at the scat. "This region is known for supporting populations of pine martens, wolverines, and Pacific fishers."

Saad shifts suddenly. "Oh," he says. "Disgusting."

"Sorry, I had to say something. My head is filled with this stuff and I never get to let it out."

"Your dad taught you that?"

"Most of what I know about tracking I learned from him. The rest I picked up from this app." I hold out my phone. "See? Scat shaped like folded cords? Weasel family."

In my head I picture a mink, which is built like a wiener dog but moves like a spring.

"That's really cool," he says. "When I was a kid, my parents took my sisters and me to the mountains in the north of Pakistan. My youngest sister was born in Kashmir. Those mountains, they looked a lot like this. The weather was the same, too. My *baba-jaan* came with us. He'd take us out very early in the morning when it was still cold and dark. I miss those days. It's not easy to travel there anymore."

"I'm sorry," I say.

"I like it here," Saad says.

"Dead bodies notwithstanding."

We wait for some rangers and the sheriff to show up. We sit still. We don't touch anything. I reapply my all-natural bug repellent for something to do. It's been unusually warm the last few days and the arthropods are waking up. A breeze sweeps over the mountainside and the branches of the two trees near us creak as they shift around.

In my head I plot trajectories, drawing lines from the rocks up the slope, trying to figure out where they fell from. Using the small pair of binoculars hanging around my neck, I scour the hillside for signs of disturbance, where the rocks may have bounced or slid before landing in their final resting places. There's a small ledge along the incline that looks ideal to launch rocks from. I can't see from where I sit because of the angle, but I'd bet a million Bigfoot dollars that there are signs of a recent disturbance in the soil up there. I think back to shotput or pitching a baseball. If someone hurled rocks at Rick Driver, they would have had to dig their foot, the right if they're right-handed, into the ground to toss rocks that distance.

Saad and I take snacks out of our backpacks and eat, facing away from the body. We drink water and look out at the forest, all the pointed tops of pine trees. It's almost like a picnic or a date, if we can just keep concentrating on the scenic vistas looking down the side of the mountain.

Behind us, Ted circles the body, as though by looking at it from different angles the whole picture will become clear. Moira is careful to stay in one place. She turns and looks down the mountain, scanning the bare canopy that is still a month away from full bloom.

Eventually, Sheriff Watkins and a round deputy with a square head and short black hair come up through the trees, with the superintendent we met earlier accompanying them.

"The Serious Accident Investigation Team is still an hour out, Ranger Cassavetes," the superintendent says, and Ted nods.

Sheriff Watkins approaches the body, examining it from head to toe, then looks up the mountain and all around. When he spots us his gaze lingers a moment, then he turns to his deputy. "This isn't ours until they say it is, just keep the scene until the chief investigator gets here," he says. The sheriff then walks casually over to us, his eyes on the ground in front of him. The incline isn't too steep, but it requires some vigilance. Carelessness can get you killed out here. He waves to us from a few feet off and keeps his arm in the air until he closes the distance. "So you decided to show up after all," Sheriff Watkins says to me.

"Excuse me?" I say.

"The town council couldn't track down your father, so we sent you his special invitation to be the guest of honour at the Bigfoot Festival. But we never heard back from you."

"I'm sorry, I never received it."

"Uh-huh," he says. "So, want to tell me what you saw here?"

"Well, we were looking for —"

"I know why you came up here, just tell me what you saw."

"We just came up the ridge," I say.

"'We' being you four?" Sheriff Watkins says.

"Yes. Ranger Cassavetes was leading, I was behind him. We came up over the ridge and we found the body."

"What were your first impressions?"

"My first impression was that this man was dead and he had been killed deliberately."

"Why would you say that?"

"The scene just gave off that impression," I say. "I know I'm not qualified to make that call. You asked and I answered. However, if I had to bet, I'd say you'll find evidence of someone having stood on that ledge right up there, chucking rocks down."

I point up to the ledge, shielding my eyes from the sun.

"Do me a favour and keep that to yourself," Sheriff Watkins says. "I don't need a panic up here because some tourist just saw her first dead body."

"That's not fair," Saad says.

"Life's not fair, kid. You see anything that struck you as peculiar about the scene?"

"No," Saad says, shrugging his shoulders.

"I see," Sheriff Watkins says. "Then it's in the hands of the rangers and the BLM. But, when they're done with you, swing by the station. I'd like to get your statements in writing."

He tips his hat to me then walks back and speaks quietly to his deputy. They both turn to look at us — I can't hear what's being said — before breaking like football players from a huddle. Sheriff Watkins then walks up to the superintendent and it looks like he might poke him right in the chest. "It's time to get serious about this rescue operation," he says.

"How do you mean?"

"I think one body is enough." He steps so close to the superintendent that they must feel each other's breath.

"And what do you suggest?" the veteran park ranger says coolly.

"Call your bosses back in D.C. and get them to put some choppers in the air; you can afford it," Sheriff Watkins says. "Driver might've been a bit of a lowlife, but what happens when a university professor winds up dead in your park? Won't do wonders for the tourism industry, will it?"

"This Driver guy must not have been popular, even when he's dead people have nothing nice to say about him," Saad whispers, leaning over, his shoulder touching mine.

"Well, he's popular enough that the sheriff could ID him on sight," I say. "But what I can't figure out is, why does the sheriff want our statements? This case is out of his jurisdiction."

"You tell me. I feel like I'm starting *Game of Thrones* at season three," Saad says. "Is this where your dad caught Bigfoot on tape?" He makes a sweeping gesture toward the peak of the mountain.

"It was farther up, just over the ridge," I say.

"And only Professor Sorel, you, and your dad know where it was shot?"

I nod. Saad leans back a little, then slouches forward, suddenly concerned that he might roll off the back of the log. He scans the area right to left.

"Then how did Rick Driver end up out here?" Saad asks. "I mean, in this exact spot. It's a long ridge."

"Good question," I say.

FIVE

At that time I had never heard of Sasquatch.
So I asked what kind of an animal he
called a Sasquatch. The Indian said, "They
have hair all over their bodies, but they are
not animals. They are people. Big people
living in the mountains. My uncle saw the
tracks of one that were two feet long. One
old Indian saw one over eight feet tall."

— Interview with Albert Ostman,
Sasquatch: The Apes Among Us,
John Green, 1978

A FOUR-PERSON TEAM OF INVESTIGATORS arrives just as Saad and I polish off a can of Pringles. Like a
meerkat colony, they all stand attentively, surveying the
scene from the mouth of the trail, trying to get a sense
of the complete picture. The leader is a man with curly
black hair with a dusting of white over the ears. He's
wide at the shoulders and looks both tough and kind.
He is followed by a lady who looks kind of like Fran

Drescher from *The Nanny*, a guy carrying a tripod, and a pink-skinned farm boy. Hands are shaken, pleasantries and names exchanged. Sheriff Watkins disappears down the hill while his deputy stays on and keeps watch.

The sun reaches its apex and begins its journey downward in the sky. I was sweaty earlier, hiking up the incline, but now that I've been sitting on the log motionless for the last hour and a half, I feel chilly, and zip my fleece up all the way under my chin. The SAIT people take pictures and measurements. They kneel down and inspect the body, then put yellow markers in the ground next to the rocks I suspect played a part in Rick Driver's death. The team leader gives more directions, then makes his way toward us slowly, like he hasn't a care in the world.

"Sorry for keeping you around," the leader of the SAI team says. "My name's Dale Jordan. I have to ask you a few questions. It shouldn't take too long."

"I don't know how much we can help you," I say.

"You were up here searching for …" he says, looking down at his notepad, "Professor Berton Sorel?"

"Yes, sir. Professor Sorel is an old family friend, so I came here to help out in the search. We have reason to believe that Professor Sorel came up here the day he went missing."

"No one seems able to account for the deceased's presence up here," he says, more to himself than to me. "Any idea why he was out here?"

"I suspect he was here for the same reason as Professor Sorel, trying to retrace the route my father and I took when we first came up here."

Dale surveys the scene from his new vantage point. He's doing some math in his head, some kind of complex calculation. You can see it in his face. He forgets that we're even there.

"Is there anything else we can do?" I ask.

"What? No. Thank you for your help. Ranger Cassavetes will take you back down the mountain. Please stick to the trail you came up on."

"What about Professor Sorel?"

"I'm afraid I can't have you hiking around this accident scene."

Ranger Ted stands behind Dale with his arms crossed, like an impatient father picking up his children. They nod at each other as one passes the other. No words are spoken.

The three of us walk down the mountain. Moira is gone, I don't see her with the SAIT people. Once again, Ted leads, I follow, and Saad watches my back. All three of us are quiet, thinking our morbid thoughts and watching the placement of our steps.

"Look," Ted says. "Don't worry about your friend."

We walk the rest of the way to the truck in silence. The flat faces of exposed serpentine rock loom above us, perfect platforms from which to rain stones down on us. Failure hangs around my neck and shoulders like chains. I sit in the back of the truck and stare at the headrest of the passenger seat.

SIX

My first impression was of a huge man, about six feet tall, almost three feet wide, and probably weighing somewhere near three hundred pounds. It was covered from head to toe with dark brown silver-tipped hair. But as it came closer I saw by its breasts that it was female.

— William Roe, sworn affidavit,
August 26, 1957

ON THE OUTSIDE, THE ROANOKE COUNTY sheriff's station looks brand new. To the left of the door are three flags hanging limp on their poles: the Stars and Stripes, the state flag, and the flag of the sheriff's department. The crest of the sheriff's department is painted in green on the door. Above the doorway, in the tiny gap between the red brick and the steel frame, pieces of straw stick out like bushy eyebrows. House sparrows fly in and out, chirping constantly. There was a time when they were only birds to me; now I register them as an invasive species, stowaways from England who accompanied our ancestors. They're notoriously aggressive, forcing native species from their burrows. When the famous naturalist Aldo Leopold wrote of this region, all he could talk about was the invasive species colonizing this land as the settlers did.

At odds with the exterior, the inside of the building feels like a bank. It smells like a bank. The deputy behind the front desk is tall and gaunt, with sunken eyes and acne scars on his cheeks. I tell him who we are and he asks us to wait, so Saad and I sit down in the line of armless plastic chairs. We face a wall covered in plaques and photos of people — mostly men — in uniforms, shaking hands with people — mostly men — wearing suits. The skinny deputy tries to look busy. I can't see what he's up to behind the counter, but I hear paper shuffling on his desk, the occasional clicking of his mouse.

"Miss Reagan," a woman's voice calls from down the hall.

Looking up, I see a female deputy coming down the hall toward me. I stand up to find she's a few inches shorter than me and about a foot wider. Her eyes are wide and brown and have an unblinking, no-nonsense look to them; her shiny black hair is tied back.

She leads me down the hall, away from Saad, and into an interview room that, despite its name, is neither intimidating nor unnerving. For one thing the chairs have arms and comfortable padding. It looks more like the waiting room at a dentist's office.

"Sheriff Watkins wanted me to follow up with you about the statement you gave earlier today," the deputy says. "You said something about the death not being an accident?"

"Yeah, I know. I'm not sure why I said that, I shouldn't have, it was thoughtless."

"So you're changing your mind?"

"I guess. I don't know enough about crime scene investigation to make statements like that. It's just, well, the whole thing looked wrong."

"Wrong how?"

"The conditions for a rockfall were all wrong. The incline of the hill, the dry conditions, even the angles at which the rocks hit the soil. They seemed to fly straight down from the mountaintop; then, as Mr. Driver's footprints climbed diagonally upward, the craters left by the rocks seemed to follow. What are the odds that rocks landed only where he'd been standing? You'd expect rocks falling randomly to fan outward, unless funnelled together by the geography of the mountainside."

"You sound convinced."

I notice her makeup for the first time. It's subtle, just a touch of eyeliner, some lip gloss, a little concealer.

"I could be wrong. There was a body lying there. I may have jumped to conclusions or missed something. I'm not an expert."

"The sheriff asked that I convince you not to spread panic and rumors in town, but I don't have to worry about that, do I?"

Her uniform, her authority, makes her seem older than she is. She gives off the impression that she served overseas, but I can't back that up with any observable facts. It's just a feeling. She speaks to me like a teacher or even the principal. Part of me thinks that I am just like her in a parallel dimension.

"No, ma'am," I say.

She smiles for the first time, twists a pen around in her tan fingers.

"Sometimes I think we try to find a reason in everything. The idea of rocks just falling loose and hitting a person in the middle of the wilderness seems just too random, right? It's natural to think there was a motive, a reason. But these things just happen, trust me."

"Have you seen anything like this? Bodies just turning up in the woods here?" I ask.

Her smile disappears. She sets the pen down in front of her and stares at it. She rolls it forward, then back again.

"Okay, that should be enough," she says. "Thank you for coming in."

"You're welcome," I say. "Have a good day."

My hand is on the stainless steel doorknob, cool to my fingertips, when the deputy speaks again. "Just for my notes, you didn't tell those government people any different than you told me, right? You didn't say anything about your previous suspicions?"

I look up and to my right, so she thinks I'm really concentrating.

"Nope, they just asked what I saw, which was nothing."

"Great," the deputy says. "Thanks."

Saad is waiting exactly where I left him. He looks up at me with no expression on his face, but his big brown eyes are always comforting.

"They've finished with you?" I ask.

He nods. "We're leaving?" he asks.

"I don't want to stay here a second longer," I say.

Saad is quick to his feet, holding the door and staring down at the tile flooring.

"Are you okay?" I ask.

Saad stays quiet and lets the door slip from his hand as he clears it.

"Saad?"

"Yes, I'm fine."

"Really?"

"Really."

SEVEN

Investigating the persistent barking of his dog at night, Dan came face to face with a hairy giant who, according to Dan, was tall and muscular, prowling in the nude. He was covered with black hair from head to foot except for a small space around the eyes.

— *Lethbridge Herald*, March 3, 1934

WE PASS OVER THE RIVER ON THE WAY BACK from the sheriff's station. The sun is ducking behind the mountains and its last, red rays seem to set the river on fire. The sawmill is a haunting silhouette, like a phantom invisible to the eye but caught on film.

By the time we get back to the motel, Saad and I are running on empty. Bats flutter around at the edge of the parking lot, just out of reach of the buzzing fluorescent lights. There's a damp, earthen smell, an atmosphere like the moist soil and moss are peeling away and all the corpses buried just beneath our footsteps will be revealed. I feel like I'm in a zombie movie — a European zombie movie, showing corpses in a later stage of decomposition, maggots squirming in their eye sockets, haunting synth music playing.

"Excuse me," a lady says in a Georgia accent. She trots along the walkway in front of the motel, intercepting us before Saad can turn the key. Her hair is like a grey clown wig; around her neck is a scarf of a thousand colours, and her earrings are of polished jade and look like June beetles. "Are you Laura Reagan?"

"That's me," I say.

"My goodness, it's an honour. I'm so grateful to your father for helping to spread the truth about Bigfoot. My name is Sylvia." She pauses and looks at Saad, who is frozen by the door. "And you," she says. "Aren't you lucky to have such a beautiful young lady as this?"

"We're not —"

"They'll never catch him, you know," she says.

"Catch who?"

"Bigfoot."

"Oh," I say. "Why is that?"

"He's not some monkey eating bananas out there in the woods. He is much more than that. So much more."

"I'm not sure what you mean."

"He's an elemental spirit. The Indians have known this all along. But you know how blind scientists can be. 'There are more things in heaven and earth than are dreamt of in your philosophy.'"

"Are you a very spiritual woman, Sylvia?" I ask.

"Haven't missed a day of church since I was yay high," she says, tracing a line at knee level. "And I never go far without my Bible." At this, she smiles and gives a little wave, turning away to walk back to her room. "Well, it was lovely meeting you."

I want to fall face-first on my bed, but Saad, shoulders back and posture perfect, walks with poise toward the back of the room as though he's completely recharged his batteries between the sheriff's station and here. He pours himself a glass of water, then offers me one of my own.

"*Paani chai-yay*," I say in Urdu, as if I am the one asking him if he wanted water.

"*Jee-haan*," he says, smiling. "*Paani chai-yay*. I like your accent."

"Thanks," I say, embarrassed.

"So, you're a celebrity now."

"Me? No. That's my dad, and only around here."

Saad furrows his brow, hesitates for a second, then speaks. "I know a fair amount about the Bible, much of it has influenced the Qur'an, but what are elemental spirits?"

"No idea. And I don't think they're in the Bible."

I fall backward onto the bed, roll onto my side, and take my phone from my pocket. A quick Google search answers our questions. Saad sits and waits for the information. He knows me well enough now — *googling* is not just a word in my vocabulary, it's a lifestyle choice.

"Elemental spirits were categorized in the sixteenth century by the philosopher Paracelsus, who divided mythological beings by the four elements. This idea was further distilled into the figure of the wild man, like a Greek satyr, which became a popular figure in European art. This figure was heavily influenced by Silvanus, the Roman god of the woods."

"Weird," Saad says.

"And pagan," I say.

At this point, Saad, ever dutiful, informs me he has to call his mother. I try to calculate what time it must be in Karachi, but I'm too tired to think. He doesn't show it, he doesn't even look at me, but I know part of him is keeping an ear out for me, wary of any sounds that might betray my presence. The last thing his mother needs to hear is the sound of a woman in her son's motel room at night. Does she even know he's in a motel room? I have no idea what she knows, what he's told her, even if he will.

"*Asalaam aleikum, Ammi-jaan,*" he says. "*Aap kesi hain?*"

I can still hear his voice faintly as I pull the door shut behind me. The night air is warm. It is the first night this year that's comfortable, past those transitionary days of early spring when it only gets warm, say sixty degrees, at midday, before dropping back to the midthirties at night. I take the time to enjoy the stars, so many of them, so many more than in the city. They look like they all might be moving, or like the current lighting them up is unsteady. I miss the stars. Camping with Dad, when the sky was so bright and clear I could see satellites orbiting above me.

"That was one hell of a day," a voice says behind me.

It's the man from the Rotary Club yesterday — the one in the suit, who'd been leaning like James Dean against the wall with his hand surgically attached to his phone. He approaches along the walkway between the motel doors and the gravel parking lot. Leaves are starting to reach out over the edges of the planters on the wall, but none come close to mussing his carefully gelled hair.

"We all wanted to go into these woods and find a body, but this is a bit much," he says.

"Pardon me?"

"I mean Bigfoot. Who doesn't want a carcass they can parade in front of the scientific community? Nobody wants Rick Driver's body."

"News travels fast," I say.

"It's my job to know these things, I have a lot riding on them."

"Who are you?" I ask.

"Sorry," he says, looking down at his shiny leather shoes and smiling. "Sometimes I think everybody knows who I am. My name is Danny LeDoux. I'm from NatureWorld. I'm here to troubleshoot for the network and make sure we get our show to air."

"That doesn't look so likely now."

"There's always hope," he says. "I'm mulling over the idea of changing Dr. Laidlaw's role on the series."

Suddenly he claps, waking me up.

"I have an idea," he says, his eyes bright like the fluorescent tube lights above us. "You could take over for Driver. A second-generation squatcher like yourself."

"I'm not —"

"I know you're not a squatcher, not really, but we can play that up. Your whole hot nerd, internet science queen thing works, though."

He reaches into his jacket, then gives me his business card.

"I wasn't aware you know —"

"Who you are? Of course I know."

"Your talent for interrupting people you just met is less than charming."

"You'll get used to it," he says. "Life's too short."

"I think your audience will be disappointed if they expect Rick Driver and they get me."

"I don't think they'll care. All they're looking for is a validation of their preconceived beliefs. That's why we trip all over ourselves to create the next *Ancient Aliens* or *Ghost Hunters*. Nobody tunes in to see 'experts.' They just want to feel like their superstitions and hare-brained ideas have scientific merit."

"Not interested," I say, just as his phone rings and he holds it to his ear, illuminating his face in white light.

"Excuse me," he says, holding a finger up to me.

The NatureWorld crew are all hunkered down in the Golden Eagle, just up the highway, same as Aunt Barb. So if Danny LeDoux isn't staying at the Tall Pines, why's he creeping around the parking lot? It's a mystery, but too minor a mystery and I've had my fill. Danny turns and faces the road, plugging his left ear with his free hand. I slip back inside the motel room, trading the sounds of one phone conversation for another.

It's ten forty-two when a nightmare jolts me awake. I can still see Rick Driver's body looking up at me from the darkest corner of the room. I can feel it lying on the floor next to my bed. My head is filled with entirely unscientific thoughts.

Silently, catlike, I creep over to the door and turn the deadbolt. Saad, cocooned in his comforter, doesn't stir as I step outside and pull the door slowly behind me.

Two men stand by the corner of the motel, next to the window where the neon vacancy sign sits. One of them is leaning against the stucco wall, smoking a cigarette. The other gesticulates in front of him, like a bird of paradise dancing to impress a mate. He sounds like he's hissing, but as I get closer I can discern the words he whispers.

"I … I only saw it for a split second. It was up the hill, behind us. I heard something, I don't know what, I must have, 'cause I turned and saw it, backlit by the sun. The creature bounded behind some trees, then it was gone."

"What did it look like?" the smoking man asks.

"It was covered in fur the colour of straw, and it was big, at least seven feet tall," the other man says. "It couldn't have been a bear, it moved too quick on its hind legs."

The smoking man looks over at me. The other one stops moving, then he, too, turns and looks at me over his shoulder. They don't say another word and I keep walking. The whispers start up again as I round the corner.

Closer to the road, the night is quiet. The midsummer songs of frogs have yet to begin. I walk along the shoulder of the highway, facing the oncoming traffic. There's a restaurant and bar not too far down. It has a painted sign on the roof, but I can't make it out from the road until I get closer. *The Paul.* In the window next to the neon open sign is a picture, made up entirely of LEDs, of a lady sitting in a martini glass. It looks like something made by a father playing with his kid's Lite Brite. Moths crawl up the wall and around the light above the door. I can hear the faintest flutter of their painted wings. Through the windows the room has an amber hue and looks lively.

The dining area consists of five circular tables in the Olympic ring formation, booths on the right and the bar on the left. The closest table to the door is full, all heads turned toward a man sitting with his back to me. I know who it is by the voice, the only English accent in town.

"I find the matter of this creature's bipedal striding gait to be the most fascinating part of this discussion. If we look at the two major schools of thought from what I call the 'physical Bigfoot' camp — that is to say, the creature is a flesh-and-blood animal with no supernatural tendencies — this animal is either closely related to us or closely related to orangutans. Now, given how dissimilar we are to orangutans, this is a fascinating dilemma."

He takes a break to sip his pint and put it down again, a ring of foam around the glass that refuses to fall back down. The one waitress in the place walks around the table, placing another round of drinks down on cardboard coasters.

"The question then becomes, did Bigfoot's hominin-like traits, such as striding bipedality, result from convergent evolution? Were these traits present in other hominids who either died out or lost them entirely? Like Orang Pendek, which may be another example of a hominin-like pongine that possesses such traits."

The room is too tight to stand around unnoticed, and some of his captive audience seems to wake up, as if from a trance, to look at me.

"Sorry, am I rambling?" Dr. Laidlaw asks, turning to follow their gazes. "Ah, Laura," he says, with a hint of an *R* sound at the end. He slides his chair over. "Do sit down."

Dr. Laidlaw introduces me to everyone and no one to me, so I sit quietly, glancing down at the laminated menu without reading it. Then he waves to the waitress and says to her, with a childlike giddiness, "Two pints of Bigfoot Brewery's Primate Pilsner."

"Sure," the waitress says, brushing a wisp of bleach-blond hair behind her ear. "Back in a minute."

"I love saying that," Dr. Laidlaw says. "'Bigfoot Brewery.' The brewery is right here in the middle of town. They have an alliterative title for every style of beer they brew: Primate Pilsner, Ape Ale, Sasquatch Stout."

"They have 'Bigfoot' everything here," I say.

"*Made from the freshest mountain waters that sustain Bigfoot himself,*" Dr. Laidlaw says, reading the slogan off a coaster.

The waitress reaches over my shoulder and drops my own Bigfoot Brewery coaster, printed with a large black footprint, down in front of me, then places the pint on it. The foam head rises over the rim of the glass and I bend at the waist to take one long sip. As the white foam recedes, I look down through pale liquid at the footprint.

"Thank you," I say to the waitress, then again to Dr. Laidlaw.

"Tell me where you stand on Sasquatch, Laura. Natural or supernatural? Hominin or pongine?"

"Assuming I believe in it at all?"

"Certainly. No fun chatting in a pub about nonexistent lifeforms is it?"

He clinks his glass against mine and takes a big gulp.

"I'm in the camp for *Gigantopithecus blacki* adapted to cooler climates by a dose of Bergmann's rule," I say.

"That seems reasonable," Dr. Laidlaw says. "But might not Allen's rule counteract the enormous height of the creature?"

He's referring to Allen's Rule, which posits that warm-blooded animals living in colder climates tend to have shorter extremities than analogues in warmer climates. This allows for a reduction in the surface-to-volume ratio. Such adaptations come in handy when you want to avoid freezing your tail off.

"We might see an increase in overall mass as a *Gigantopithecus* population migrates north, per

Bergmann's rule, but the reported long limbs of Bigfoot seem to be at odds with Allen's rule. They'd lose tremendous heat in ice age conditions."

"Moose seem to do just fine," replies a round man with glasses pushed back high on the bridge of his nose, a waxed moustache more William H. Taft than Salvador Dali beneath.

Dr. Laidlaw continues. "I am told by friends of mine who specialize in moose that you can see both forces acting on moose, depending on their distribution. In colder climates moose tend to be large, in keeping with Bergmann's rule. But bear in mind that Allen's rule applies to all extremities, not just limbs. So those northern moose also tend to have shorter ears to mitigate heat loss."

"I hate to argue against my own position," I say between sips of my beer, "but we have no idea the true size of *Gigantopithecus*. The only remains we have are a dozen molars and some mandible pieces. It might've just had incredibly large teeth for its size."

"There's another point for the true believer," the man with the moustache says. "There are only a handful of *Gigantopithecus* fossils anywhere. Conceivably, there could be *Gigantopithecus* bones somewhere in North America and we just haven't uncovered them."

"That's not the most flawed logic I've ever heard in a pub," Dr. Laidlaw says. "But then there's the question of diet. According to Ciochon et al., opal phytoliths found on the surface enamel of *Gigantopithecus* teeth shows that the animal ate a variety of grasses and fruit, distinctly different from the plant life found in this habitat."

The table becomes silent as we consider Dr. Laidlaw's comment. I look above our table, at the light fixture. It's made from an old wagon wheel and suspended from the ceiling by chains, a black cord snaking over the links and powering the amber lights. Half a dozen of these lights, like a fleet of flying saucers, shine down over the heads of the squatchers. Maybe there are some locals here, too, but from the looks of the crowd I'd say it's mostly people taking up all the motel rooms and eating all the Bigfoot breakfasts.

"I find the supposed smell associated with Bigfoot to be a fascinating feature of the lore," Dr. Laidlaw says. "Many members of the lemur and loris families coat themselves with pungent substances as a defence mechanism. Perhaps the majority of bears and wolves, even humans, would avoid the creature due to the odour alone."

The man wearing a newsboy-style flat cap chimes in. "I find these crossovers between the Sasquatch legends and real-life primatology so fascinating. There's the matter of the odour, like Dr. Laidlaw points out. Then there's the issue of the shoulders getting in the way of the Sasquatch turning his head, as Dr. Grover Krantz observed in the Patterson-Gimlin film."

He's some kind of naturalist and writer. His waxed moustache and tortoiseshell glasses are right out of the twenties. All that's missing is a cigarette holder squeezed between his teeth, which he indeed might own. You can never tell in a non-smoking environment.

"Daniel is the author of the *Bigfoot Researcher's Field Manual*," Dr. Laidlaw explains.

"I try to use the interest in Bigfoot to teach people principles of field biology," Daniel says. "Plus you put Bigfoot on the cover of a science book and it'll sell much better."

"Hear, hear," Dr. Laidlaw says, raising his pint glass.

A heavy-set lumberjack look-alike peels away from the bar and makes his way out the door. With him out of the way, I now see Ranger Ted Cassavetes is at the bar, doing shots and chasing them with beer. He notices me looking and raises his glass to me. His blond stubble, golden in sunlight, looks dark inside the bar. Ted bent over and drinking looks like a film noir anti-hero drowning his sorrows.

"My word," Dr. Laidlaw says. "I do think I've drank back all the calories I lost on the search today." He slides his chair back — it squeals against the hardwood floor — and surveys the landscape until he finds the washroom, then walks around the other tables until he gets to the dark, narrow hall at the back of the Paul.

The waitress comes by and asks if I want another pint of beer. I look at the time, then shake my head. "Better not," I say.

Moments later, another pint appears anyway. I look at the waitress with subtle incredulity.

"He insisted," she says, pointing a thumb over her shoulder.

Ranger Ted leans back on his stool and waves. He now looks less like the down-and-out noir detective and more like a silly frat boy.

"Excuse me," I say to the rest of the table, before getting up and walking over toward the stool next to Ranger Ted.

"Hey," he says, raising his glass.

"Hey," I say back.

"Everybody comes to the Paul," he says. "It's the only bar in town."

"I'm not really in the drinking mood," I say. "But thanks for the beer."

"I heard about your little debrief at the sheriff's station. Don't let Watkins or his goon squad bother you," he says. "He's just worried about his job."

"Is it an election year?" I ask.

"There's a push to amalgamate three of the smaller sheriff's departments around here. If that happens, Watkins won't be top dog anymore and he'll ride out his term in office giving out parking tickets."

When he notices me looking at the shot in front of him, he conceals it in his meaty fist. He knocks it back the next time I look away, then slides the empty glass across the bar, as far away from him as he can reach. The bartender picks it off reflexively as he passes.

"Last thing Watkins will want is a major crime that might expose the shortcomings of his department," I say. "Especially if it's a journalist like me who reports the crime."

"Oh, it's worse than that. A murder on federal land? That would automatically bring in the FBI. People might start asking whether we even need a local sheriff around here if a regional outfit can do more and cost less."

"A man lost his life and local politics take precedence."

"Sheriff Watkins has been a bigwig around here since I moved to this town. Even before that. He doesn't know how not to be the boss," Ted says before emptying his glass. "Look, Laura, I'm sorry I was hard on you before."

"It's cool, we sort of got off on the wrong foot," I say. "Stressful situation."

"Let me buy you a drink."

"You already did," I say, pointing to the half-empty pint glass on the bar.

"Okay, one more," he says. "You deserve it."

"It's been a long day," I say. "My tolerance isn't what it should be. I'm afraid if I drink any more I'll be no good in the search tomorrow."

Ted's blue eyes pool with a kindness I didn't think he was capable of.

"That's fair," he says. "You're really worried about this professor of yours, aren't you?"

"He's like a grandfather to me," I say. "I don't think I'd have become a science journalist if it wasn't for his encouragement."

"You work for a newspaper or something?"

"I run a website dedicated to communicating science to the general public. It's a skill that's sorely underpractised."

"So you write for an online *National Geographic* or something?"

"My site is like any other news site, except it covers science stories exclusively."

"How did you get into that racket?" Ted asks.

"I started a Facebook page in university called Science Is Awesome, where I reposted science news stories and press releases from academic institutions. I even started designing my own infographics for the page. When it took off, I decided to launch my own website and here I am."

"And you make money off this?"

"I do."

"Good money?"

In my parents' day that would have been considered a rude question.

"Very good money, all things considered."

"Wow," he says, looking at the bartender and signalling for another pint.

"Do you always power drink like this on a week-night?" I ask.

"Only when I find a dead body," he says. "So, your website. Is it like your career now?"

"For the time being."

"What does that mean?"

"I'm not sure it's my calling. It grew so fast that I struggled to keep up. I've been too busy slipping punches to counter, or even to think about going on the offensive."

"'Slipping punches'?"

"You don't have the monopoly on boxing analogies," I say.

"I don't know too many girls who use them."

"You should get out more," I say. "I don't know why

we're even talking about this at all. I don't usually talk about myself so much. I guess I'm just ..."

"We're going to find him, you know that, right?" Ted says. "We'll find him and in a month or so you'll forget this ever even happened." He takes a long sip of his beer, draining half the glass in one go. "You won't forget me, of course," he says, wiping his mouth with the back of his fist. "You'll never forget me."

"You know your one shortcoming, Ranger Cassavetes?" I say. "You lack self-confidence."

"I know it seems that way," he says, smiling. "I'm just humble to a fault."

"Tell you what," I say. "You find Professor Sorel, and I'm not likely to ever forget you."

"Deal," he says, offering his hand.

I take it, and shake a little. Ted doesn't let go. He's getting comfortable with the contact, too comfortable. "I should go and get some rest," I say. "It'll be another long day tomorrow. Hopefully one where I can spend all the daylight hours searching."

"Let me walk you home."

"That isn't necessary."

"I'd like to," he says. "Plus now I feel guilty. I should go home and sleep so that I can start fresh in the morning."

"Bright-eyed and bushy-tailed," I say.

"Affirmative."

• • •

The first thing, the only thing, we hear when stepping out into the cool spring air is the sound of the Klamath River flowing invisibly in the blackness of night. I stop and take a second just to listen. Even though it's a block or so down the street, it sounds so near, as if I'm standing on the bank. Ted stands shoulder to shoulder with me, or at least my shoulder to his biceps given our height difference. He's listening, too.

"I think of the Klamath like a nomadic army, marching from the plains in the east, set on invading the Pacific. Every tributary is like another band of mercenaries joining the cause," Ted says.

"You watch a lot of History Channel?" I ask, smiling.

"History books are the only books I read," he says, though I'm not sure if he's embarrassed or boasting.

We walk along the main street, which is mostly dark except for the street lights and the old, one-room movie house. THE ALPINE, in red neon lights, blazes diagonally across the front of the theatre. The marquee, a constellation of glittering incandescent bulbs, reads THIS WEEKEND: BIGFOOT DOUBLE BILL: HARRY AND THE HENDERSONS/THE LEGEND OF BOGGY CREEK 1PM/7PM.

"I love these old theatres," I say. "I'm surprised a town this small has one."

"It's the only one within miles of here," Ted says. "When it was built, back in the thirties, people came from all over the state, even northern California and western Idaho and northwestern Nevada. A few years ago, when it changed ownership, the new management wanted to change the name to something

Bigfoot-related, but the town council protested it unanimously and the new buyers backed down. That's the only time when the name *Bigfoot* was prohibited from being slapped on the front of a business in this town. The Alpine is just too important. This place is legendary. We should see a show while you're here."

"I don't think I'll have time," I say.

"Not much else to do here in town," Ted says, taking a step closer and eclipsing the street light above me.

"I should be getting back," I say, stepping away.

"Oh, yeah, sure," Ted says.

We turn north, back toward the motel. Up the road a fox crosses from the shadows into the yellow glow of the street light, then back into shadows again. A slightly overgrown bush waves as it passes, the only evidence the fox came through there at all.

"Hey," a voice calls from behind us.

Three men stand under the Alpine's marquee. Ted steps forward, half shielding me. "Stay behind me," he whispers over his shoulder.

I don't need him standing up for me. They aren't dangerous-looking, they're almost pathetic. Plus, all it would take is one forceful shove to knock him back against me, then we'd both fall, end up on the concrete, and find ourselves in incredible danger. I move like a knight on a chessboard, to the side and forward, to get around him.

"Yes?" I say to the men, ignoring Ted. "Can we help you?"

The leader of the trio comes forward, the street light shining down on his long brown hair and matching long, catfish-like moustache. He wears a denim jacket, a white T-shirt, and jeans, like he was dressed on an assembly line in the era of Bruce Springsteen, John Mellencamp, and Jon Bon Jovi. His friends, similar in age and style, hang back.

"You the two who came across Rick Driver's body today?"

"Yes, sir," Ted says.

"We wanna know what happened to him."

"Rock slide," Ted says.

"Bullshit," the man says. "Someone got him."

"It can be dangerous hiking up on the mountain during the spring thaw," Ted says.

"We want to see the body."

"Ask Sheriff Watkins in the morning," Ted says. "He's an agreeable fellow."

"He won't tell us nothing," the man says.

"We can't tell you anything either," I say. "There's nothing to tell."

The man, probably drunk, just stares at me a while, not even blinking.

"I'm sorry about your friend. He was an old acquaintance of my dad's," I say.

Finally, the man blinks, then nods. "Let's go boys," he says. He turns around and walks back between his friends. Like loyal underlings, the other two wait for him to take the lead before the three of them walk away. Ted watches them distrustfully until they cross the street in front of the drugstore.

"Nice work," Ted says.

"Thanks."

"And thank you for not mentioning murder, or any of that stuff you said on the mountain."

"Why would I? I am not an idiot."

"I know," he says, hooking his thumbs into his pants pockets like he might line dance down the street. "Was your dad really a friend of that Driver guy's?"

"Apparently, they knew each other. Driver said as much yesterday. I can't corroborate it."

"Well, now that that's over, can I walk you back to your motel?"

"No thank you," I say. "I'll be fine on my own. I'll see you tomorrow."

"You won't let me protect you, will you?"

"Who says I need protecting?"

Ted chuckles a little, then straightens up and smiles.

"Good night, Laura."

"Good night, Ranger Ted," I say.

EIGHT

America's first Sasquatch-catching expedition headed into the mountains of British Columbia to-day on a hunt for the horrible, hairy naked bogey-man of Indian legend.

— *Fresno Bee*, April 9, 1934

THE ROADS ARE SLICK FROM RAIN THE NIGHT before. The moss, clinging to roadside rocks and carpeting the soil between trees, glows vibrantly green.

We arrive in a convoy with the rest of the search and rescue volunteers. Another day has passed and the hope is ebbing. Word of Rick Driver's death has worked through the crowd of volunteers. It worked on them all of last night, and now the urgency to rescue a live man is fading into the duty of recovering a dead one. They march out together, solemnly, their heads hanging low. I don't let it get to me.

Word is also spreading about the Bigfoot sighting that took place yesterday. A foursome of volunteers, none of them the men from the motel last night, repeat the story. I linger just a second to listen.

"Do you believe that? Henry saw Bigfoot."

"He did not."

"That's what he says. Saw him yesterday, just north of the road that winds around Roanoke Ridge."

Ranger Ted, wearing a look of concern, weaves between the volunteers, on an intercept course with us. He doesn't have a pack on. Crows caw in the trees to the right of the road.

"Hi, Laura, Saad," Ted says. "Glad to see you made it home safe last night."

"Good morning," I say.

"What happened last night?" Saad asks quietly, looking at me.

"Nothing," I say.

"Roanoke Ridge is off limits today," Ted says, "until the SAIT guys are gone and are sure there's no threat to anyone else, no volunteers are allowed."

"What about Dr. Sorel?" I ask.

"After that little blow-up with the sheriff yesterday, my boss decided to request an aerial SAR unit out of Medford to scan the whole area with FLIR cameras. We'll be working with the other volunteers searching the rest of the park and river valleys."

"I should be up there," I say, then realize how arrogant I sound.

"We tried it your way, as a favour to Dr. Sorel's wife.

But now the man's been missing for over forty-eight hours. Another man has been found dead. We really need to bring out the big guns here."

"Fine," I say. "We'll take whatever section you want us to search and we'll search it."

"Great. Moira's been moved to another group but I'll accompany you guys. We've been assigned the far side of the mountain, near the hot springs."

Ted leads, consulting his GPS. We follow a dirt road on foot, part of a parade of volunteers that grows smaller and smaller as we go. I hardly notice when we're the only ones left.

A creek runs next to the road, on my left. On my right, a hill rises at a sharp angle. Bushes, shrubs, and small trees dot the hillside. The exposed dirt is dry and resembles sand. This patch of land resembles Nevada more than Oregon — the price of a drought, I suppose.

There's a well-worn trail leading up the steep hill-side, a tail of dirt strewn downward that sticks out because the dirt is a lighter colour than the surface soil around it. It leads up to a tunnel carved into the side of the hill, too clean and wide to have been made by an animal. The walls are too flat and the top is too arched to be natural. It resembles a tiny doorway out of *Alice in Wonderland*.

Ted shields his eyes from the sun and takes a long look at the tunnel. Exposed roots have been hacked away and the dry, stiff husks of last year's shrubs have been ripped from the soil. "There shouldn't be any active mines in this area," he says. "Nothing on the maps anyway. Probably an old claim that someone's scavenged recently."

"Should we check it out?"

"We'd better," he says. "Would you like to do the honours?"

Halfway up the hill it occurs to me that he suckered me, and now he's down below, hands over his eyes, checking me out. I glance over my shoulder and see the back of Saad's head. He's put himself between Ted and I, and seems to be making conversation or asking questions.

The dirt around the mouth of the tunnel has been disturbed recently, just before last night's rain if I'm reading the signs correctly. The tunnel itself is a little tight, even for me. I want to be able to turn around quickly and move easily should I have to, so I take my pack off and lean it next to the adit. I also take out my emergency kit and some glow sticks, stuffing them into the oversized pockets of my cargo shorts.

My LED flashlight fits perfectly in the palm of my hand. The ghostly white beam I shine into the darkness diffuses long before it hits the back wall of the mine. The tunnel seems to lead all the way to Seattle. The timbers above and beside me have rotted away and look like burnt matchsticks.

"Hello?" I call out. "Professor Sorel?"

I bend at the waist and slightly at the knees, and enter the tunnel slowly. Partway in, I reach into my pocket, feel the smooth surface of a glow stick, and draw it like a dagger. I put the flashlight down for a second to crack the glow stick, shake it until I'm bathed in its ethereal amber glow.

"Professor Sorel!" I say one more time.

I toss the glow stick as hard as I can and watch it travel the darkness like a firefly. It lands softly, noiselessly, in the well-trodden dirt. I shine my light around some more, in a circle, starting from the floor to the wall to the ceiling and around.

There's a little sliver of colour on the ground, something out of place. Lying in a swirl of loose sediment is a sliver of thin plastic, the colour of milk chocolate on the outside and with a reflective foil on the inside. I smell it. There's still an odour of food, so it's recent. I look around for more signs of human habitation, but there's nothing.

"Anything?" Ted calls out from the mouth of the tunnel.

"Just the corner of an MRE wrapper."

"Is it fresh?"

"I'd say so," I say. "Brisket Entrée, from the smell of things."

MREs, or Meals Ready to Eat, are a staple for any soldier. They seem to have certain addictive qualities, too, based on how Dad could never fully wean himself off of them. When we'd go camping he had some quota, unspoken but certainly in his head, of food we needed to gather from the wilderness, whether it was fish, blueberries, or just pine needles for tea. The rest of our meals were supplemented by MREs. They had fewer flavours back then, and I never found them particularly good, but like instant noodles or mac and cheese from a package, there was something comforting about them. Dad flipped out if I wanted to bring a bag of Oreos along, saying *your body doesn't need that crap*, but he had no issue with cheese tortellini in tomato sauce out of a package that looked like plastic explosives.

"Could've been left by a miner," Ted says.

"That's possible," I say.

"We'll mark it down on the map and keep moving."

I do one last sweep of the area with my flashlight. Maybe if it were bright enough I could find another clue, something to confirm the professor had been here or something to eliminate that possibility entirely.

Backing out of the tunnel, I slip my pack on again and we continue our search. Overhead and off to my right a helicopter flies in a search pattern. Birds chirp in the sumac trees growing out of the side of the slope, picking at the dried bobs — the fruit clusters — to find the nutrients that are always in season.

Back at the bottom of the hill and up the road a little, Saad stands by an outcropping of rocks that make a perfect spot to sit and eat. Granola bars and a package of trail mix get passed around. The drumming of woodpeckers provides a soundtrack, along with the sounds of us gulping down water from stainless steel canteens. We have a good three hours of hiking ahead of us before calling it a day, so a moment's rest and food will go a long way.

Ted leads the way as we move in the shadow of Roanoke Ridge, the beating rotor of the search helicopter cutting into the sound of birds and the distant voices of other search parties. A hundred people have to be scouring this park, not to mention the helicopters, but standing here at the foot of a mountain and among a vast expanse of trees, I can't help but feel helpless, like we are searching for a needle in a field of haystacks. I don't like the feeling and we push on.

Saad, unaccustomed to a strenuous day of hiking, demonstrates his exhaustion — all his little aches and pains — in the slow, Frankenstein's-monster way he's walking. The search and rescue helicopter breaks off its search and flies off overhead toward the airfield in Medford. One more day is done and we're still no closer to finding Professor Sorel.

A crowd forms south of the ranger station, near all the parked cars. There's a commotion. Ted pauses, taking the scene in. One man's voice rises above the chorus.

"They got footage! They caught that bastard on tape!"

"Show us," a voice calls from the crowd.

I press forward and Saad follows. Ranger Ted hangs back with his arms crossed, a professional look of disinterest on his face. It's a melee, which is hardly a surprise given that the bulk of the volunteers are here for the Bigfoot Festival.

A phone is held up cautiously, and the video plays.

From my standpoint, there is nothing to see.

"I can't see it," someone says.

"Post it on the forum!" a voice yells.

"Here," the owner of the phone says. He climbs up on the back of his pickup and sits on the tailgate. He holds his phone to his chest and plays the video again, looking like a kid doing show and tell. His smile tells me that he's enjoying his fifteen minutes of fame, he's feeding off of it. We still can't see anything. I give up and Saad follows.

Ranger Ted has an I-told-you-so smile on his face as we approach him. "Is that the definitive proof of Bigfoot?"

I ignore his comment. "Ted, can you find out what grid they were searching?"

"Do you think it'll help find your professor?"

I ignore his mansplaining tone, too. I don't need to be reminded of my missing mentor.

"It might," I say. "But don't ask me why. I guess it's just too much weird for one time and place."

I can't help but think that if there is such a thing as Bigfoot, now is the time we'd find it. Search parties on the ground, helicopters in the air, the odds of finding it are better than ever. One can't imagine a squatching expedition, or even a primatological one, with this many resources.

"It'll be pretty warm tonight," Ted says. "If your professor is as well equipped as you think, he'll be fine." He squeezes my shoulder reassuringly.

I can't place this guy, he's all over the map. One second he's arrogant, condescending. The next he is sweet, sympathetic, with a look in his eyes that tells me he will tear this area apart looking for Professor Sorel, if only I'd ask.

NINE

Texas oilman Tom Slick is going after the
Abominable Snowman — with blood-
hounds and a helicopter.

— *Lethbridge Herald*, August 2, 1956

SAAD HAS TAUGHT ME ONLY THE MOST
rudimentary Urdu, so as I listen to him speak to his
mother I can only pick out words like *yes* and *no*, as
well as *okay* and *mom*. She is waiting for him to pick
a career, to settle in one place, to have a steady pay-
cheque on which he can support a family. From there,
marriage and children. He tells me she keeps an ear
to the ground for eligible bachelorettes from good
families, she tries to introduce him to these good
families at every opportunity. It shouldn't bother
me, but it does.

I search every Bigfoot forum I can think of until I
finally come across the footage shot earlier today. It's a

shaky, typical blob-squatch video, no discernable detail except the blur is the colour of dry grass. There's no shape resembling anything. The audio, unlike the picture, is clear: Footsteps crunching over the dry brush. The sounds of excitement and "look-it" and "there it goes" that fit perfectly into the film.

"*Allah hafiz*," Saad says, hanging up the phone and dropping it onto the bed. Turning to me, he says, "Want to check out the Bigfoot Museum?"

I look at the clock in the bottom corner of my screen; it's six thirty-seven.

"Won't it be closing soon?"

"Extended hours," he says. "For the Bigfoot Festival."

"Nice," I say. "It beats sitting around here."

The Roanoke Valley Bigfoot Museum and Gallery is more subdued in scale than something, like, say, the Guggenheim. It's a hybrid of the great American roadside tourist trap and some kind of religious shrine.

The doors are guarded by two Sasquatches carved out of wood. They stand just over six feet tall, which is taller than me, but seems a little short for Bigfoot. Sitting on the gravel by the door, as if in worship of one of the statues, is a young man with unnaturally orange hair and black ear gauges. There's a canvas knapsack on the ground beside him, flap open, revealing a gaping pocket. He's sketching the statue on the left, his pad lying across his knees.

Saad lingers, and the artist looks up at him, his expression half-flattered, half-*do-you-mind?* "That's really good," Saad says.

"It is," I say, backtracking and taking a second look.

"Thanks," the artist says.

"Are you in town for the Bigfoot Festival?" Saad asks.

"I sure am. I came all the way from Vancouver for it."

"Washington or B.C.?" I ask.

"The real Vancouver," he says. "B.C."

"Are you an artist?" Saad asks. "Or do you just sketch for fun?"

"I'm hoping to drum up some interest for my comic." He reaches into his knapsack and pulls out a graphic novel with a glossy cover that glimmers in the sun. He holds it out between us. The title is *Sasquatch: Guardian of the Northwest.* A Sasquatch is on the cover, one foot up on a rock, a log held high above his head. Underneath is the artist's name, *Andrew Price.*

Saad takes it from him and flips through it. Drawn across the panels is a story about a Sasquatch disrupting the construction of a pipeline that is supposed to transport fossil fuels from the tar sands in Alberta to the Pacific coast. The news here covers the Keystone XL project more, but I know in Canada there are several pipeline projects that draw protests from the Indigenous Peoples of the region and activists. Both groups would definitely benefit from having Bigfoot on their side.

"This is good stuff," I say.

"Do you read comics?"

"Sometimes," I say. "I still read *X-Men* from time to time, but mostly I just read indie stuff now."

Saad looks over at me with astonishment. "I didn't know you read comics."

"I'm selling this for twenty bucks," Andrew says. "Want a copy?"

Saad considers this for less than a second and nods. He passes me the comic while he fishes out his wallet.

"How long did it take you to do this?"

"About a year," he says.

"Wow," I say.

"Yeah, I have some sweet software to help with the layout and the colouring, but still."

"I'll take a copy," I say.

"I only have the one on me," Andrew says. "I'll be selling more at the book table during the festival."

"Cool," I say. "I'll swing by."

When we walk into the museum, there's a rapid onset of darkness that my eyes need to adjust to. The proprietor behind the counter snaps quickly to life to welcome us inside. With his long white beard and bald scalp he resembles Charles Darwin post-*Origin*.

The museum is empty, which is strange. Any given weekday, sure, but we're on the eve of the Bigfoot Festival. The place should be packed.

The museum seems intended for the casual visitor passing through on their way north to Seattle or south to San Francisco, but once I'm inside, I see the museum is clearly designed for the true believers. Whereas at most major museums across the country it is common to read the words *palaeontologists believe that* or *fossil evidence suggests*, here there is no room for skepticism, for anything other than absolute certainty. The deeper into the museum you travel, the more it becomes an echo chamber of Bigfoot belief.

Though small lights on the ceiling light up particular exhibits, the museum is dim and smells like an antique store. The first thing we see is a glass case mounted on a pedestal, a spot fit for the rarest medieval Bible. Inside is the issue of *Argosy* magazine containing the first coverage of the Patterson-Gimlin film. A placard on the wall provides four paragraphs of context about the film, which was shot on October 20, 1967, a short drive from here down Interstate 5. It's perhaps the most watched and most iconic piece of eight-millimetre film ever shot, next to the Zapruder footage of the Kennedy assassination.

The next exhibit is entirely dedicated to the Roanoke Ridge film, my father's film. Built into the wall is a small television. A white plastic button sticks out from the wall under the screen. Around it, on the walls, are blown-up still frames.

Saad, almost reflexively, takes a short step forward and presses it. The black screen turns blue, then it is filled with static. Finally, the film begins to play.

I could describe the film with my eyes closed. It's shot from somewhere down the mountain facing upward. The sun creates lens flares as the camera pans over to a cluster of white bark pines growing out of a mossy carpet on the mountainside. A log on its side, bleached by the sun and bone-like, occupies the centre of the frame. There's some kind of movement. A bipedal, fur-covered creature lumbers out from behind a grouping of trees on its way toward an outcropping of rocks. It seems to gesture down the slope. Then, a smaller creature rises up from behind the log. They both move out of the frame, their locomotion obscured by the branches and the rocks that Sasquatches always seem to move behind. The whole video isn't even thirty seconds long.

Beside the film exhibit is … a mural? An infographic? A poster? I'm not sure. It's a crudely put together image of three lifeforms: a chimpanzee, the Sasquatch from the PG film, and a white man wearing nothing but a loincloth. There are thick black arrows connecting the three beings, starting from the chimp and moving through to the *Homo sapiens sapiens*. The words *Missing Link?* are written above the Sasquatch.

"Guess they're not worried about staying up to date," I say, quietly, looking down the length of the museum for the long-bearded proprietor.

"I can't even remember the last time I heard someone use the term *missing link* in reference to human evolution," Saad says.

"It's like a great slogan, I guess. It really sticks in the brain. I think it has broad appeal, makes discoveries of transitional fossils more appealing to casual readers of science stories. But it's an idea that's as outdated as most of the stuff on these walls. The chimpanzee-human last common ancestor is a thing. The *missing link*? Definitely not a thing. If I used that term in an article I'd have a legion of biologists and anthropologists banging down my door with torches and pitchforks."

"That would make a good story for the site."

"It certainly would. I'm sure the entire scientific community wishes the term would go extinct. The word *link* implies a chain, which refers to the Great Chain of Being, a pre-Darwinian religious notion of the hierarchy of all life. But there's no hierarchy. Life is a tree that branches out in all sorts of fascinating directions."

On the wall in the next room is an old front page of the *Klamath River Tribune*. A black-and-white photo of Sheriff Watkins is dead centre, holding the cast of a Bigfoot print. The headline reads: *Bigfoot is Out-of-Season, Permanently*. Watkins is twenty years younger in the photo, his cheeks jagged and his moustache — now a snow-capped mountain — a solid black strip above his lip. The plaque below the image outlines the creation of the ordinance that prohibits the hunting of Bigfoot within the Roanoke County limits. Saad reads the story and chuckles.

Stone ape heads line a shelf built right into the wall. The heads are carved from a variety of stones that have natural apelike features and were found in the Columbia River. Squatchers see these as proof that the Natives of the region have encountered Bigfoot in times past. I hardly think stones with atavistic traits form concrete proof, but at the moment, the town is full of people who'd disagree.

Saad and I leave the cavernous museum and walk out into the waning sun. This time of year it doesn't get dark until eight. The ground beneath our feet is all well-packed dirt and stones, and when the wind kicks up only a very thin layer of dust from the surface rises and sweeps across our shoes.

As we walk, a passing truck stops abruptly, reverses, then turns into the museum's parking lot.

It's Ranger Ted. He pulls up close, looks through his open window, hesitates, then gets out. "The SAIT guys have picked up and left," he says.

"Okay," I say.

"They've called off their investigation," he says. "The death of Rick Driver no longer seems accidental."

You don't say *I told you so* at a time like this — not when a man has lost his life — but for a career fraudster like Rick Driver, it's okay to think it.

"Did they say why?" I ask.

"No, not to me anyway. They just packed up their stuff, spoke to my boss, and called in law enforcement. Officially, we're keeping this quiet, especially 'cause the Bigfoot Festival brings a lot of tourists through this town and we owe it to the locals not to start a panic."

"But you told us," Saad says.

"I told Laura. You just happened to be here," he says, then turns to me. "You were right. I still think it was a bit of a fluke, considering it took seasoned investigators a day to conclude what took you thirty seconds, but you were right all the same."

On the way back to the motel, we drive past the Paul and notice a crowd gathered in the parking lot. A man in jeans, white sweater, and green vest stands in the back of a pickup truck and speaks to the crowd. We can hear his voice but not his words.

"Should we pull in?" Saad asks.

"I was just thinking that." Last time we joined a crowd like this, we caught a glimpse of "Sasquatch."

The man is red-faced and his voice is starting to break. Sweat is visible on his brow and mats his hair. We both get out of the car and close our doors quietly to not interrupt him.

"I saw it with my own eyes," he says. "The government folks picked up the stakes and left. The sheriff is in there now."

"That don't make it murder," a voice in front of us calls out.

"It sure means it was no accident," the man replies.

I recognize the man in the truck from the other night. He was the leader of the trio, the one inquiring about Rick Driver. How he found out about the departure of the SAIT people is a mystery, but it's no surprise he's here now. He reaches down into the crowd and pulls up the man we saw earlier who filmed the Sasquatch while searching for Professor Sorel.

"We know there's something out there, this man took a video of it!"

The crowd looks expectantly toward the man, but he says nothing, just scratches his elbow while seeming to count every face in the crowd.

"Go on," the man in the vest says. "Tell 'em, tell 'em what you saw."

"Uh … well … we were coming back from searching a valley behind Roanoke Ridge, on the far side of the mountain. The sun was setting and we had to get back to the ranger station. Then we heard it, whatever it was. It wasn't a big noise, just a little clicking noise. I was last in my group and kept looking over my shoulder. That's when I saw it move. It was huge, camouflaged in all that bush. We locked eyes for just a second, then it took off, westward through a thick patch. Man, could this thing move. It leapt over rocks and logs like an Olympic athlete."

"We're going to find this creature," the man in the vest says. "And we're going to find it tonight! The meetup will be at ten, at the end of Burnt Creek Road!"

The crowd cheers like this is a stump speech. It seems a little too orchestrated, too convenient. Saad and I walk back to the car.

· ● ·

Back in our motel room, we eat pizza for dinner and watch the movie *Double Indemnity* on Saad's laptop. I text Ted, thinking he'll back out of the Bigfoot hunt. To my surprise, he replies with a thumbs-up emoji, followed by *see you at 9:45*.

There's no relaxing. I count the minutes and feel my pulse rise. I look out the window and find a police cruiser in the motel parking lot. The windows are down and there's no one behind the wheel. Someone comes out the door of the manager's office: the deputy who interviewed me at the station two days ago. She is scribbling something in her notepad, the floodlight above the parking lot shining on her dark hair tied back in a bun. She glances up at my window and I wave. She nods at me, scribbles some more, then a look of recognition comes over her face.

"Hey, Deputy," Ted calls out, appearing out of nowhere and crossing the parking lot. The deputy's rigid posture and stiffened jaw muscles relax, as though she is deflating. She smiles and seems to not know what to do with herself. "Hey yourself, Ranger," she says.

They both half turn as they pass each other. Then Ted's smile disappears. I never thought he would be that calculating.

"Good evening," he says, when I answer the door.

"Hey, Ranger," I say.

"Don't you start," he says.

We both watch the deputy's cruiser pull out of the parking lot, pause for a passing lumber truck, then turn out onto the highway. She's visible in profile, looking down the end of her nose at the road. It looks like her hair is tied back so tightly it might snap.

I turn to Ted. "How's the investigation into Rick Driver's death going? Any idea?"

"I can't say for sure, but I hear things. The FBI has taken over the investigation since the crime took place on federal land, but they've bent over backward to make the sheriff's department feel included, probably because of those gun nuts in the next county who think every federal employee is part of a covert invasion."

"Sheriff Watkins must love that," I say.

"Except all this investigation is doing is highlighting his ineptitude. He can't even find where Rick Driver was staying. Plenty of people can place him in town up to two days before his death, but none of the local motels have him in their registries and his pickup is nowhere to be found."

When Ted follows me in, Saad looks at us without expression and begins packing his stuff. My bag is already packed, including my flashlight, glow sticks, a camera, a video camera, a bottle of water, and an extra sweater.

I check the Bigfoot meetup site and confirm the location. Since the cellphone footage was uploaded, all the squatchers in the Pacific Northwest have been making their way out to Roanoke Valley.

"Are you ready to hunt Bigfoot?" I ask.

* ● *

"This is a bad idea," Ted says, sitting down in the back of our rental and pulling the door shut behind him. "If any of the guys find out I came with you, I'll never live it down."

"I wouldn't be too worried, if I were you," I say.

"I thought you came out here to find your professor, not hunt Bigfoot."

"One experienced woodsman goes missing, another is killed in the same area, and now there are these sightings? I can't believe that these are isolated events."

Ted, leaning forward, peeks around the fabric-covered headrest at me. He sits back and exhales. "A lot of crazy stuff happens — it's not all related," he says.

"It's this or sitting around my motel room, praying your helicopters find Professor Sorel," I say. "Unless you can pull some strings and let me back on the mountain."

"Point taken," Ted says.

A dozen cars line the grass at the side of Burnt Creek Road. An odd combination of smells wafts and whirls together in the air: bacon, peanut butter, even anchovies. There are a dozen recipes for the "perfect" Bigfoot bait, none of which have ever conclusively worked.

To my surprise, there's a camera crew here. Danny LeDoux, the TV producer, stands next to a van with the NatureWorld logo on the side. He's in jeans and a blazer, the most casually dressed that I've ever seen him. He spots me, pushing his head forward like a turtle to make sure. I wave and he waves back, then knocks on the sliding door of his van. It opens and a man wearing a backward baseball cap, polo shirt, and khaki shorts pops out.

"I didn't expect to see you here," Danny says.

"You thought the roaring nightlife of Roanoke Valley would sweep me away?"

"Mind if we tag along with you?" he asks.

"I'm not going on camera," Ted says. "No way in hell."

"We won't use any footage without getting you to fill out a consent form," Danny says.

"You won't tape me at all," Ted says. "I want to keep my job."

"Okay, Ranger Smith, you're out," Danny says, turning to the cameraman. "No face time for the ranger, here, Chris."

The cameraman gives a nod and a simultaneous thumbs-up.

"Ranger Smith. From *Yogi Bear*," Saad whispers to me, responding to the look of confusion on my face.

Lon Colney is here, too, wearing an outfit right out of Indiana Jones. He stands at the mouth of a logging road that splits off from the main road and curves around the mountain, watching the group in silence as backpacks are slung into place, flashlights turned on, battery packs on camcorders checked and rechecked. A semicircle forms in front of him as the faithful, the veteran squatchers, stand at attention. The rest of us follow their lead.

Lon speaks. "As always, be careful out there, folks. One man has already died out here and another is missing. Look out for yourself and the person next to you. Respect the land and each other, and please, don't wander off alone."

The squatchers fan out like we're on a scavenger hunt at summer camp. Saad, Ted, and I stay together. Danny LeDoux and his cameraman, Chris, follow along behind us, sticking close to each other.

Although it seems like the ideal starting point, we keep away from Roanoke Ridge. Nobody wants to be caught disturbing a crime scene — we're lucky the sheriff's department hasn't shut this thing down already.

Ted leads us down a logging road that curls around the base of the mountain. We get far enough in and the bush on the left falls away as the hillside tapers and drops into the stream that looks black in the darkness. Voices carry on the wind, getting quieter and quieter as the squatchers separate. We rest on an outcropping of rocks, leafless branches stretching out overhead, and look across the valley as though from a sniper's nest. Maybe it's just the night-vision scope. There are definite advantages to teaming up with well-heeled TV producers. We pass it around like college kids smoking a joint.

Suddenly, a loud bass call explodes from a cluster of fir trees across the valley, near the crest of the hill. It sounds like a demonic version of Tim "the Toolman" Taylor's grunting. Through the night-vision scope I can see three men standing together. The middle one is cupping his hands around his mouth and making the call. The bass rises into something like the Johnny Weissmuller Tarzan yodel, then into the sound a diva would make if you pulled the shower curtain back on her. There is total silence, then the squatcher calls again.

I peel away from the scope and look off in the darkness, up at the stars, at the trees on the ridge that are black silhouettes against the night's sky.

From somewhere farther up the mountain, a bellow erupts, unlike anything I've ever heard. I look back at the squatchers who made the first calls. At first they're frozen, then they split up. Two start ascending the mountain, the middle one stays behind, making his call again then listening for a response.

Ghostly white flashlight beams shine through the trees, then start to converge as different bands of squatchers cross paths to follow the sound. Their lights look alien on the mountainside. Shouts echo from one side of the valley to the other, rolling over the ridge and through the trees. The beams of flashlights shine through the leaves, cutting swaths through the night like lighthouses off-kilter. I hear branches snap, dry brush crunch, the heavy thuds of boots running over dry soil.

"There! He's there!" a man yells.

The flashlights start to coalesce — they've found a focal point. A cluster of men climb up onto the ridge, moving across it in a line chasing something that we can't see.

"Follow me," Ted says. "We can take this trail back to the road and cut off whatever they're chasing."

He breaks out into a sprint, the beam of his own flashlight swinging side to side like a pendulum. I follow like a distance runner, conserving energy, moving cautiously, always keeping one eye on the terrain in front of me and the other on Ted. My ears search for Saad constantly. I hear his steps, his laboured breathing behind me. Danny and Chris hang back. The beam from the LED top light on Chris's camera diffuses as I run beyond it. Danny gives instructions but I can't make them out.

The starlight is enough to navigate the dirt road. Ted switches his flashlight off and I see his blue shirt clearly. We've managed to head the squatchers off at the pass, like we're in an old cowboy movie. The gaggle of flashlight beams are coming down the ridge and heading straight for us, deviating only where the men holding them encounter obstructions, rocks and trees to climb around. A branch breaks and something heavy slides down the hill in an avalanche of dead leaves.

Ted clicks his light on and does a sweep of the area immediately next to the road. I use my beam higher up on the hillside and Saad adds his to the effort. Ted walks a little farther up the road and I follow, gesturing at Saad to stay put. Danny and Chris stay behind me and to the right. We're casting our net a little wider. The men on the ridge have slowed down, trying to climb down the hill without falling.

"Who has the scope?" I whisper over my shoulder to Danny and Chris.

My own natural night vision is horribly inadequate. Each amorphous blob could be a creature in a crouch, each branch could be an arm outstretched. A white LED beam hits me dead in the chest and works its way up. One of the squatchers is almost down to the road. The beam lifts up a foot and I'm blinded in its glare.

"Who's there?" a man's voice asks.

Bushes part and I hear feet on gravel. The beam pulls off my face and points to a section of road between Ted and I, just as a hairy figure crosses the road and dives into the trees on the other side, evergreen boughs snapping back in protest.

It all happens in the blink of an eye.

I can't even be sure it was real.

I take a step to pursue when I feel a tug. Someone has grabbed the handle at the top of my backpack.

"Laura —" Saad says.

In my peripheral, I catch the glimmer of a pistol. The muzzle spits out fire and the sound cracks the night. A cry of pain from somewhere in the woods freezes the squatchers in their places for a split second.

Ted closes the distance between himself and the gunman and, not slowing his own momentum, snatches the pistol from the man's hand before knocking him flat on his ass. "Are you out of your mind?" Ted shouts. "You could have killed any one of us." He ejects the magazine from the pistol and puts it in his pocket. Then he draws back the slide three times, making sure the chamber is clear. "Is everyone all right?" he asks.

"Oh, come on!" Danny says when he sees Chris lying on top of his camera, the lens separated from the body of the device.

"Sorry," Chris says. "I saw the gun and backed up, must have tripped on —"

"Give that back," the gunman says. In the ambient glow of all the squatchers' flashlights, I recognize him as the man from the Paul, the one who brought this whole thing together.

"Come by the ranger station in the morning and you'll get it back," Ted says.

Three or four people, uninterested in the drama playing out in the middle of the road, shine their lights into the woods where the creature fled. The branches have settled now, leaving no sign of commotion. A lithely built man, dressed head to toe in camo gear, peers into the woods — then, as if seeing the perfect moment, jumps in after the creature. One other person follows before I join the fray.

I have to confirm what I saw. I just have to.

"Laura!" Ted calls out.

Saad says nothing and joins the pursuit. We are not on a trail, not even a game trail. In a month or two the greenery will be too thick to effectively pursue anything faster than a tortoise. I hold my flashlight in an icepick grip, like a cop, with my right hand. My left is cupped on the top of my head, my elbow pointing forward, blocking the branches from snapping back and hitting me in the face.

The trees part into a gully carpeted with moss and dead trees in various states of falling over. All varieties are here, from rotting logs to diagonal-pointing woodpecker targets to trees perfectly upright but with no buds on their branches, the kind that don't even realize they're dead. The two squatchers in front keep moving, following a sound from the trees ahead.

I pause and shine my light on the ground. The moss is like a memory-foam mattress from those TV commercials, recording almost perfectly the imprints of whatever stepped on it. There has got to be a sign that something other than people has passed through here, but I see nothing but boot prints larger than my own.

"Stay back," I say to Saad. "Please."

Again he adds his light to mine. I take my phone out of my pocket and use the flashlight feature to increase the brightness. Saad follows suit and soon I have enough light to get a decent picture of the immediate vicinity.

Poking up through the soil is a rock wearing a moss toupee. Down the centre of the moss is a thick, syrupy puddle that appears black in the glare. I take a few pictures before putting my phone away, then use my pocket knife to amputate the moss.

"Saad, could you shine your light over here, please?"

I tear the cardboard front off my notebook, slide it under the sheet of moss, and put the whole thing into a Ziploc bag.

As we climb back up to the road, we see headlights coming from the opposite direction of the main road. It's a convoy of jeeps. They stop in perfect synchronization, as if one brain is controlling all three. The lead jeep's passenger door opens and a man gets out, then walks around the front of the jeep, eclipsing one headlight, then the other. He wears a uniform like that of Special Forces, the desert camo kind, and has a pistol strapped to his thigh.

"What's going on here?" he says. "We heard a gunshot."

The gunman, still dusting himself off, points to Ted. "He stole my gun," he says.

The other doors open and more men get out, forming a line behind the first man, who assumes the stance of a commander. They wear the same uniform and are also armed.

"Who are these guys?" Saad whispers.

"I don't know the specific group, but they're some kind of patriot group, like the Oath Keepers. Right-wing militias who tend to butt heads with the federal government over local land use and property rights," I say.

"I didn't steal it, I confiscated it," Ted says.

"And by what authority did you confiscate this man's firearm, and thus violate his Second Amendment rights?" the commander asks.

"I work for the Forest Service," Ted says. "He discharged a firearm dangerously close to civilians, with no regard for public safety."

"Have you learned your lesson?" the commander asks.

"Yes, sir," the gunman says.

The commander turns to Ted. "I think you ought to return to this man what is rightfully his property."

"That's not your call to make," Ted says.

"Did you hear that, gentlemen?" the commander says, turning to his men. "This forest ranger has declared himself a one-man Supreme Court."

"I'm enforcing the law," Ted says.

"Enforcing the law? Is that what you federal boys are doing, taking over a miner's claim and burning down their shacks, and on what? Technicalities. I'd call that piracy."

"I served in Iraq and Afghanistan," Ted says. "The rule of law is all that stops America, or any country, from turning into a war zone. You boys think you're bringing freedom with all those guns? That's exactly what the Taliban think. All you're bringing here is chaos. Now why don't you back off so I can do my job."

The commander, his hands behind his back, walks up to Ted, stops a foot away. He tilts his head back, clearing the bill of his hat from Ted's face, and looks down his nose at him. It's almost like the commander is breathing him in. "Nice speech, now give this man his weapon back."

"My dad always said, give in to a bully once, you'd better be prepared to give in to him for the rest of your life."

"Your daddy and me would have gotten along just fine," the commander says. "What would he think about you?"

"My dad is proud of the man he raised."

"Here," I say, slipping the pistol out of Ted's waistband and handing it to its owner. "Take the stupid thing."

"Smart lady," the commander says.

"Why don't you and your men get back to doing whatever it is you do," I say.

"Move out, boys."

The men get back into their jeeps and we all take a few steps back to clear enough space for them to make U-turns. Their tail lights burn like demonic eyes in the darkness as they disappear through the winding dirt road. The tension pours out of the bystanders as the standoff comes to an end.

"What about the ammo," the gunman says.

Before I know what I'm doing, I kick him in the balls with a full-speed front snap kick. "You stupid son of a bitch. It wasn't bad enough you fired off your gun right next to my face, but then you snitch to some militia guy? Are you out of your mind?"

The rage subsides and I feel Saad and Ted holding me back by either shoulder.

The gunman is looking up at me, his eyes conveying both fear and pain. "Did you see that?" he says after several deep breaths.

The crowd disperses. Nobody saw anything, and they are going to keep it that way.

Behind us, the bushes part. The two men chasing the Bigfoot have returned, winded, bending at the waist and resting their hands on their knees.

"He's hurt, he's definitely hurt, but he still got away," one of them says. "No man can move that fast wounded like that."

TEN

Gathering material for a book, (Roger) Patterson talked to many old-timers and residents in the Trinity Mountain Alps area. Reports were gained by him of people who had seen the creature. Most descriptions concur that what Patterson is after is a creature which is tall, hairy, and apelike …

— *Union-Bulletin*, September 23, 1966

BACON SIZZLES ON THE GRILL BEHIND THE counter. A waitress passes our table with a plate in each hand, then slides them along the neighbouring table-top to hungry patrons already holding their cutlery. The other waitress walks over with the coffee pot, re-filling our cups.

The TV in the corner is playing a morning show out of Portland. The scene changes from a man and a woman sitting around a table in a studio to an aerial shot of a forest and a mountaintop. The banner at the bottom of the screen reads *Bigfoot Attacks on Roanoke Ridge?* The scene changes again. A young man in a well-fitted suit holds a microphone in front of a backdrop of trees. The breeze that shakes the branches behind him does nothing to his short, well-gelled hair.

I ask the waitress if she can turn up the volume.

"I'm here on County Road 12, not far from the scene of a grisly murder, a murder committed by what locals are saying was a Bigfoot."

The camera switches to a wider angle and we see the man with the gun, the man who I kicked in the groin, looking wildly at the reporter. He doesn't once look over toward the camera. He's jittery. Ben Compton is his name, according to the caption at the bottom of the screen.

"Can you tell us what happened here?" the reporter asks.

"My friend Rick Driver was volunteering as part of a search and rescue operation when he was killed by a Sasquatch. It threw stones at him. They do that, you know, they throw stones, great big ones. Remember Ape Canyon? Well, this one killed Rick, and the Forest Service is trying to cover it up!"

We see some shots of previous Bigfoot Festivals as a voiceover sums up the armchair squatcher's history of the region. "In 1924, in a canyon near Mount St. Helens — an area a lot like this one — a group of miners were pinned down in a cabin by a group of what they described as ape-men, who hurled stones at them. The miners bravely fended them off, potentially killing one of these beasts in the process. The area was later named Ape Canyon after the incident."

Back in studio, the two hosts trade inane remarks about the idea of Sasquatch. The woman ends with a comment about staying out of the woods and locking her door at night, while the man finishes by saying that his, and the network's, thoughts and prayers go out to Rick Driver's family.

Saad straightens up a little, looking over my shoulder. I follow his gaze and see Sheriff Watkins removing his aviator sunglasses and scanning each of the faces in the diner. His eyes lock on mine and he points to me as though he's pressing a particularly stubborn button. I slide out of the booth, putting my hand on Saad's arm to stop him from coming with me.

"Stay here, it's probably nothing," I say. "If for some weird reason I don't come back, tell Ted what's happened."

"Laura," Saad says as I walk away.

When I reach him, the sheriff does an about-face and goes for the door, holding it open for me like a proper gentleman. "Did you tell that idiot Compton that Driver was killed?" he says quietly.

"No, Sheriff. This is just the sort of thing I wanted to avoid."

"Smart girl."

"Smart enough to deserve an explanation?"

"About what?"

"That SAIT guy, Dale Jordan, why does he think Driver was murdered?"

"They found evidence, on the ledge, right where you said they would. Not footprints so much as … impressions, of something having stood there. Something man-sized, I might add. All the rocks by the body had been pulled out of the ground from that spot. This was no spring thaw accident."

"I didn't want to be right," I say.

"I heard about what you did last night," he says. "That was assault."

"Is Compton pressing charges?"

"No, but he doesn't have to. The State can, since we can make a strong case without a complainant. But if it were up to me I'd give you a citation." The sheriff tries smiling at me but it doesn't come naturally to him. "These cowboys that you met last night," he continues, "are a danger to regular folks and their everyday lives. Last thing I need is an army of out-of-town yahoos coming here armed to the teeth telling us what the law is, using intimidation in place of authority. And that weasel, Compton, I'd lock him up for shooting a gun off in a crowd. But if I did that I'd have to throw you in the cell beside him." He looks off at the empty lot across the highway. Gravel with weeds poking through, a wall of hemlock trees in the back. "I knew your father, I'm not sure if you knew that," he says, turning to study my face.

"I didn't."

"I can't say I like a lot of the Bigfoot hunters that come through here, but I liked him. He cared about this town. He didn't just come here looking for Bigfoot and to hell with the rest of it. He had a sense of duty."

My face does something, I'm not sure what, but Watkins picks up on it.

"I don't know what kind of man he was as a father or a husband, but here, he was the kind of man you could count on."

"Sheriff?"

"Yes?"

"When my dad came here, was Rick Driver ever with him?"

"Sure, that whole crowd came around here then, just as they do now. I remember the three of you together, sitting at that picnic table, eating ice cream."

He points down the highway. I can see the picnic table, and the building with a walk-up window and a big ice cream cone–shaped sign.

"You were just a little girl then. It's no wonder you don't remember." He takes a step closer to me, tilting his chin down and looking through bushy eyebrows at me. "I think it's best you steer clear of the search today. Not much you can do anyhow, and I think you should lay low before Ben Compton swears out a complaint against you. From what I hear, your ranger friend has been given the day off, too. The Forest Service doesn't want to court any more controversy than they already have."

"I can do that, Sheriff."

"Good girl," he says. "There's one more thing I was going to ask you. We'd like to notify Driver's next of kin and collect his personal effects, but we haven't been able to locate where he was staying. I know you don't remember much of the time he and your dad spent together, but is there any favourite place of your father's, a cabin or trailer park, where Driver may have stayed?"

I shrug. "No, I can't think of any place. When Dad used to bring me up here we always camped right in the woods. We never stayed anywhere."

"Thank you for your time then," he says, tipping his hat to me before walking to his car.

When I get back, Saad is using a piece of whole-grain toast to wipe up what is left of the eggs on his ketchup-smeared plate. "Is everything okay?" he asks.

"Yeah, it's fine. But our plans for the day have changed."

Saad looks almost relieved to learn he doesn't have to traipse around the woods for a third day in a row.

"We need to find out where Rick Driver was staying," I say.

"Why?" Saad asks, taking the napkin from off his lap and wiping his mouth.

"There's more to this, more to all of this, than we understand. I need to know how my father's involved." I'm still coming to grips with the idea that my dad was of the same ilk as Rick Driver, a remorseless hoaxer and cheat.

Saad leans over, his elbows on the table, and speaks softly. "How can you be sure he has any involvement with Rick Driver?"

Just then, the chimes above the door announce a new customer. Dr. Laidlaw walks in, looks around for a spot, then sees us and smiles.

"Good morning, good morning, how are we?" he says.

I slide over in the booth. "Care to join us?"

"I'd be delighted," he says, sitting down. "So long as I'm not imposing."

"Not at all, Dr. Laidlaw."

"I heard there was quite a bit of commotion last night."

"I'm surprised we didn't see you there," I say.

"I was otherwise engaged, I'm afraid, recording a podcast via Skype."

He flags the waitress down and spends several minutes conversing with her until they come to a consensus of what bangers are and how he can get some, and compromising on home fries in place of mash. "So," Dr. Laidlaw says, pouring cream into his coffee, "give me all the eyewitness details. The creature, what did it look like? How large was it? Describe its locomotion. Did you manage to get a photo of the thing?"

"It came out of the brush so fast," I say. "There wasn't any time to take a picture."

"A decent counter to the argument of why we have no photographs of this animal, given that everyone has a camera on their phone," he says.

"I didn't really see it. It was just a shadowy figure on a dark road. There was no time for perspective. It was moving toward me, there were people behind me, armed men emerging from the woods, flashlight beams everywhere."

"Chaos."

"Exactly," I say.

"How about you, Saad? What did you see from your perspective?"

"I saw even less. There were three people between me and the creature, one of them a cameraman. I couldn't see around him."

"Hold on, do you mean the NatureWorld camera crew was with you? Is there a video of this encounter?"

There is a list of people who I hoped would never see the look on my face when I realize I am a total idiot. Dr. Duncan Laidlaw was certainly on that list. Now, I'm afraid, that ship has sailed.

"I never thought to ask," I say. "The camera itself was damaged in the encounter, so I just assumed the tape was destroyed, too."

"Easy enough to find out," Dr. Laidlaw says, pulling his phone out of his corduroy pants. He searches his contact list, squinting a bit and showing his two front teeth.

I listen to the *tick-tick-tick* of his button pressing. Saad's eyes meet mine and I smile; I don't know why.

"Danny? Duncan. Just having breakfast with my mates Saad and Laura. Thought we ought to ring you up and ask if you salvaged any footage of your little adventure last night. No? Not yet anyway. Defragging? Certainly. Certainly. Perfectly understandable. Quite all right, then."

Dr. Laidlaw looks at me, shrugs, then leans forward and slips his phone back into his pocket.

"That reminds me, I have a couple phone calls to make," I say to Saad. "Then let's take a little trip."

In the back of the diner, where it's quiet, I call the number I'd saved while googling all those Bigfoot hoaxers our first night in town.

Donald Oreskes answers, his voice husky. He wheezes when he gets excited, his pitch growing higher and higher, and he chuckles at the mention of my dad's name. I was prepared for resistance, but this guy just wants to chat about old times.

"Yeah, John — back then 'Rick' was still John — his dad was a bit of a boozehound, his mother didn't think it was safe to raise a boy in a house like that, so she shipped John off to live with his grandma, a lady by the name of Sally Johansson. She lived not too far from Roanoke Valley, a twenty-minute drive at most."

"One more thing, Mr. Oreskes. About the bus hoax. Was my dad the man in the gorilla suit?"

"Your dad? No. We didn't hook up with him until a year or so later. Met him in that very town you're standing in now."

Ted has offered to guide us to the Johansson house. As we follow his truck, I can see him through his back windshield, bobbing his head to the radio, his air of authority all but dissipated.

There's a nagging doubt in the back of my mind. What if we're wasting our time? If we don't find anything, how do I explain to Aunt Barb that I wasn't even looking for Uncle Berton? I rest my phone on my thigh and glance down at the screen. Should I be at her side? Right now she's sitting at the ranger station, worrying while search and rescue operations carry on around her.

We drive into a town under siege. Militia men from the next county, dressed like Special Forces, walk around with assault rifles hanging from their backs, semi-automatics strapped to their thighs. Heads turn and eyes narrow on our vehicle.

"There's practically an occupation army," I say. "It's insane."

My phone buzzes. It's Ted.

"We need to stay away from them," he says. "Please. They're dangerous."

"I have no plans to reacquaint myself with them."

"One of them shot at me two years ago. I had bullet holes in the side of my truck. He said if he wanted me dead, I'd be dead. Can you believe that? These people call themselves patriots — until their country asks something of them that they don't like, that's inconvenient maybe, then it's all get your guns and shoot at the guy trying to keep your country beautiful and free."

"What's their deal?"

"Most of them were soldiers at one point or another. Many of them are out of work," Ted says.

"Soldiers without a mission have a way of finding one. Right now they're trying to stop the government from evicting a pair of miners who violated the mining regulations on federal land. But if it wasn't that, it would be something else. Groups like this have occupied land in Grants Pass and Burns, not to mention similar actions in other states. I'm not sure what it's really about, though. I mean, so much of the West is owned by the federal government and a lot of people around here resent that. But local governments are too small and don't have the resources to actually manage this much land."

Out the other side of Roanoke Ridge, we come to a bend and stop at a driveway that is almost invisible, just two tire ruts covered over by dead leaves that curve far back from the road. There's a mailbox here, labelled JOHANSSON. Its little red flag is down and the sheet-metal structure of the box itself is browning with rust.

We drive up halfway and park our vehicles next to an old maple tree with branches that reach out over the driveway. A fence with split wooden posts, rife with knot-holes and rusting nails, stretches along the front of the property. The house itself, hidden from the road, is one stiff breeze away from collapsing. A squirrel vaults across the awning over the porch, and I can't help but think the whole structure might fall apart under its weight.

Saad and I walk toward the front door, slowing at the sight of the steps, all of which have either bowed in the centre or split completely. Ted walks around the side of the house, following the tire ruts to their conclusion.

"Guys," he calls out.

We find him standing next to Rick Driver's pickup truck and its footprint decals. Hitched to the back is a trailer large enough to sleep in. Both have Texas licence plates.

"We can tell the sheriff we've finally found where Driver was staying," Ted says. "Too bad it's out of his jurisdiction."

"If his truck is here, how did he get to Roanoke Ridge?" I ask.

"It's not too far from here if you go through the woods," Ted says. "It's just the road that curves around the park, on foot it's a straight line."

"Shouldn't we knock on the door," Saad says.

"He's right," I say to Ted. "Last thing we need is a dose of shotgun justice from someone who doesn't take kindly to trespassing."

Back at the house, Ted takes a running jump and hops all the broken steps. He reaches down and offers his hand for me. I step up on the skirt board, which looks sturdy enough, and jump up to the porch, no assistance necessary. Saad looks over the situation and decides to walk up to the porch beside the stairs, grabbing hold of the railing and pulling himself up.

The windows are frosted over with dust and grime. I knock on the door lightly, fearing the thing will fall right off its hinges. Boards creak under our feet; aside from that, and the wind whispering through the tree branches, the whole area is quiet.

"Try the door," Ted says.

I look back over my shoulder at him.

"What? We came all the way out here," he says.

"Mr. Lawman over here wants to break and enter," I say.

"No breaking, just entering."

I turn the knob, and as the door creaks open, I close my eyes for a split second, expecting a face full of buckshot. Then I step inside, Saad and Ted fanning out behind me.

"Hello?" I call out.

The inside of the house is covered in cobwebs, the air thick with dust. Moving deeper into the kitchen, I notice a wood stove against one wall, the kitchen sink against the other, and a door leading to a mud room. Only a small area around the sink and counter has been cleaned recently. Through another doorway is the dining room, with cabinets covering one wall and a big oval oak table in the centre, and beyond it are French doors that open into a den.

"If you fixed this place up, it'd be a beaut," Ted says.

In the den is a dead lynx mounted on a log, its glass eyes glazed over with dust and cobwebs dangling from the gaping mouth. In the corner, sitting on the floor, is a TV in a massive faux wood case, the cathode tube in its back the length of my arm. It's older than the TV in our motel room by at least a decade. The corners of the screen are filthy, but somebody wiped it recently, a swirling, circular area visible in the centre. Resting on top is an old VCR.

Upstairs there's a bathroom and a long hallway with two doors on each side. The ladder leading to the attic has been left down in the middle. I head straight for it, while Ted and Saad sweep the other rooms.

"We got some gear in here," Ted says. "And clean sheets."

In the attic are the gaping mouths of a hundred cardboard boxes. At the far end is a window with a sunbeam pouring through, and beneath it a long wooden trunk like a coffin. I walk immediately over to the trunk and flip the lid. Inside is a gorilla costume with the hair coloured brown instead of black.

"Sasquatch," I say. "The body found."

Ted joins me, keeping his head down to avoid bumping it on the beams.

"Well, at least we know what happened to Scott Kelly's gorilla suit."

"Not going to laugh at that," I say, remembering the video of an astronaut dressed as an ape floating around the International Space Station.

Beside the trunk there's a box of VHS cassettes, *Roanoke Ridge 1993* written on the side in black magic marker.

1993. The same year my father shot film of a juvenile Sasquatch and its parent.

"We have to take these tapes," I say.

"I know I was all about looking around in here, but stealing stuff? I'm not sure I can be a part of that," Ted says.

"Go and take a leak in the woods and Saad and I will move the stuff into the trunk."

"Do you really need it?"

No one knows where the original Roanoke Ridge tape is. Many skeptics highlight that fact alone to undermine the tape's authenticity. I've searched through a full garage trying to find where my father hid the tape. If it's here, if he and Rick Driver were together when he shot it, I need to know. I need to find that tape.

Saad drops the boxes down to me through the attic door, then climbs down. Ted walks ahead as if to maintain plausible deniability. In the reflection of the French doors I see the VCR sitting on top of the TV, like a male tiger beetle mounting a much larger female.

"Saad, grab that VCR," I whisper. "We're going to need it."

When we step outside, a grey truck slows down at the end of the driveway, then speeds up as we get closer. A carcass, mutilated by a car, is now lying at the side of the road. Three crows pick at it with all the urgency of unionized city workers.

"What is that?" Saad asks.

"No clue," I reply.

Ted studies the carcass, squinting at it from where he stands but not getting close. His mouth opens and closes again. He wants to be able to answer, to be the man with all the answers. But sometimes a dead animal is next to impossible to identify from a glance and at that distance.

When we get to the car, a northern goshawk soars over the opening in the trees. Ted looks away while we load the trunk with the stolen articles.

"We should copy all these videos to my hard drive," Saad whispers to me.

"How?"

"I don't have the necessary equipment, but I'm willing to bet that those NatureWorld guys have everything we need in their van."

E L E V E N

Roger Patterson, 34, the man who said he
photographed an abominable snowman in
the mountains of northern California this
fall, has been charged with grand larceny
involving a 16mm movie camera.

— *Lethbridge Herald*, December 2, 1967

BEFORE WE RETURN TO THE MOTEL, I INSIST
on checking in at the ranger station. It's practically
empty when we arrive. What was just, a few days ago,
the nerve centre for the search and rescue operation is
now a frontier trading post. The crime scene and the
use of helicopters in the search completely change how
the operation is being run. There are two rangers on
duty. One sits by at the comm station; the other leans
back in his chair and is tossing a water bottle up into the
air then catching it right above his stomach. He snatches the bottle out of the air and sits upright as we walk in.

Ted greets the two men. "Morgan, Karl."

"'Sup, Ted," Karl says, squeezing the water bottle.

"Did the helos turn up anything?"

"Not yet," Morgan says. "They're done for the day."

"Is the chief in?"

"No, he's taken Barb home."

"Barbara Sorel?"

"What? She insisted," Karl says. "Isn't this your day off?"

"Yeah, but these are some friends of the missing person and they have some information that might prove helpful."

We sit around Ted's desk. It's organized and sterile and mostly tells me nothing about him. There is, however, a red picture frame on the corner with a photo of a German shepherd sitting on the edge of a porch, mouth open, tongue dangling.

"Cute dog," I say.

"Yeah," Ted says. "Ralph was the best. Dad had him put down when I was overseas. Cancer."

"I never realized dogs got cancer," Saad says.

"Yep," Ted says.

There is a large map of the area on the wall to my left. Professor Sorel could be anywhere on it. It's almost inconceivable that the helicopters have been unable to pick up his heat signature.

"This whole thing is turning into a mess," Ted says quietly, conscious of the two other rangers on duty. "It should be simple SAR, but then a man gets killed. And then there's this mess with, of all things, Bigfoot.

Who'd want to set up such an elaborate hoax at a time like this?"

"That is, assuming it is a hoax," Saad says.

"I don't see any evidence that says otherwise."

"There's the bloody moss I found," I say.

"We can't be sure that it's blood," Ted says. "This whole thing could be some kind of publicity stunt. Ben Compton could've shot a blank."

"Were there blanks in the magazine when you ejected it?"

"No. But he only fired one shot. The first one could've been a blank. Think about it. If you've spent your life hunting Bigfoot, and now you believe it killed your buddy, wouldn't you fire more than one round? Especially if all you're packing is a nine-millimetre? You can't take down something the size of Bigfoot in one shot with anything lighter than a thirty-aught-six."

"There's no official size for Bigfoot," I say.

"It shouldn't be too hard to determine if it's blood or not," Saad interjects. "It's a simple enough test. I could probably find the materials in your kitchen and first aid kit to test that substance myself."

"The sample's still in the trunk," I say.

There are times when it pays to hang out with a chemical engineer.

After retrieving the sample, Ted leads Saad through the back of the office into the dark hall, yellow lights flipping on as they move room to room. I'm about to follow when the map on the wall catches my eye and makes me realize something.

Let's operate under the assumption that all the recent Bigfoot sightings were of the same thing — that there is only one individual "creature" on this side of the mountain. That's not a rational conclusion, but for my purposes it's a workable hypothesis. Let's stretch the facts a little further and assume that this creature also killed Driver. A pattern becomes clear: the creature is moving down the mountain, and at the same time away from the search grid.

"Laura," Saad calls from down the hall.

He and Ted stand in the tiny kitchenette. Saad scrapes a sample of the dried liquid off the moss and places it in the centre of a white plastic plate. He then reaches to his right and grabs a brown bottle with a white cap, untwisting the cap quickly like we're timing him.

"Fake blood in old movies used to be nothing but chocolate syrup, did you know that?" Saad asks. "In black and white the chocolate comes through more clearly on camera. Think of that great scene in *Psycho*, of Martin Balsam falling down the stairs after being stabbed, blood splatter on his face. Then movies started to be shot in colour, but blood wasn't a big problem in Hollywood because of the Motion Picture Production Code — sometimes called the Hays Code — which heavily censored American films. The British, however, used a ton of fake blood, especially in their lame Hammer films. The blood they used was either too bright, screaming red at the audience, or too dark, because many studios still shot B movies in black and white. It was Dick Smith, who worked on movies like *The Godfather*, *The Exorcist*, and

Taxi Driver, who perfected the recipe for fake blood. It's a base of white corn syrup mixed with red and yellow food colouring, methyl paraben, and a wetting agent used to develop film called Kodak Photo-Flo."

As he speaks, Saad pours the hydrogen peroxide on the blood sample on the plate. Tiny bubbles cover the sample. I feel like I'm back at science camp mixing vinegar and baking soda together while a lady in a white lab coat talks about acids and bases. For a long time, I thought it was acids and *bascids* on account of her accent.

"This is not fake," Saad says. "That's blood. The bubbles are given off by the enzyme catalase, in the blood, which breaks down hydrogen peroxide into water and oxygen. The oxygen then escapes as gas — all the bubbles we just saw."

"Let's hope it's a hoax," I say, "that this is just pig's blood or something, and Compton didn't actually hit anything. There was too much of it scattered across that trail. The animal this blood belongs to will die if it doesn't treat its wound."

"That'll be the test of how smart Bigfoot is — if he can tie a bandage," Ted says.

"Ted, do you have a map of all the mining activity in the area?" I ask.

"Of course. Why?" Ted asks, walking through the office and stopping at a filing cabinet that stands against the north wall.

"I have a hypothesis," I say, careful not to use the word *theory* frivolously.

Ted, pulling the map from its drawer and crossing the room, lays it out across his desk

"Where was the mine we searched yesterday?"

Ted stabs the map with his index finger. The mine he's pointing to, where I'd found the MRE wrapper, is right between where Rick Driver was killed and where the Bigfoot was shot.

"Hey, Saad," I say. "Remember those two wildlife documentaries, the one about wolverines in northern Alberta, and the one about Amur tigers in Siberia? In both cases, the cameraman had to hide for days in the area where these animals lived in order to become a part of the habitat, to fade into the background. They built blinds to live in, sometimes didn't leave them for days."

"Hunters do the same thing. I used to work at Grand Teton. Every year I'd have to tear down blinds after the elk hunt finished," Ted says.

"What if Professor Sorel is tracking this thing the same way? I found an MRE in that mine yesterday," I say, pointing to the map. "Mines make good blinds. They're already familiar features on the landscape. A Sasquatch wouldn't get spooked by them."

"How do you know the MRE belonged to the professor?" Saad asks.

"I don't, this is all guesswork, but it's a hunch we can test. If we find any other evidence that a man has been hiding out in these mines, it will further confirm my hypothesis."

"But wouldn't he call his wife?" Saad asks.

I shrugged. "This is his obsession," I say.

"So, if he doesn't want to be found, there's nothing to be worried about, right?" Ted says. "Sure, there'll be hell to pay for all the wasted SAR man-hours, but aside from that —"

"Something out there killed Rick Driver. We can't risk it getting Professor Sorel, too."

"So now you think there's a real Bigfoot out there? That this isn't a hoax," says Ted.

"It could be a hoax so elaborate it's fooled even Professor Sorel," Saad says.

What pops into my head, and I'd never say this out loud, is that maybe Professor Sorel has become so desperate that he can be taken in pretty easily.

"This all sounds looney tunes to me," Ted says. "So, what's the game plan?"

"We check all the mines from here to here," I say, drawing a line with my finger. "Do you think we have enough light left to check any of them today?"

"Sure," Ted says, squinting at the map. "I'd say we can make the closest."

A pair of headlights catches my eye through the window of the ranger station as a car makes a U-turn out front, heading back in the direction of town.

Saad checks his phone for the time. "What about Danny LeDoux and that video equipment?"

"Right," I say.

"I could meet him at the motel," says Saad.

"You don't mind?"

"Anything to avoid doing any more hiking or climbing."

· • ·

Ranger Ted is loose now, relaxed, not the rigid military man I met three days ago. We get into his truck and hit the road, and the whole thing seems routine.

"You're a tough girl, aren't you?" he asks, not taking his eyes of the dirt road.

"There's a limit to how much I like being called a girl," I say.

"Fine. Tough young woman."

"Depends on how you define tough."

"I mean, you can handle yourself out here."

"I was practically raised outdoors," I say. "And I train Muay Thai twice a week, and my gym offers a ladies' Krav Maga class that I attend every Sunday."

"I don't know what that is but I take it that it's some fancy type of karate."

"Something like that," I say.

"Which one of those classes taught you to nut that idiot Compton?"

"Actually, my dad taught me that," I say.

When we arrive at the first mine, Ted pulls the truck over as far as he can, wedging it into some small shrubs along the shoulder. On the other side of the road is a steep hill leading to the river below. I push my door open and face an almost perfectly vertical rock face.

At the edge of the road stands an evergreen tree with drooping branches that look like rags. The tree itself looks like the witch from *Snow White*, an eerie figure in the waning daylight.

"Brewer's spruce," Ted says, "*Picea breweriana*. It's endemic to this region and is considered a relict species. Dinosaurs would have chewed on trees just like that."

"Aren't you Mr. Knowledgeable."

"That's my job."

We start the slow climb down to the riverbank, Ted in the lead. The incline is gradual and there are plenty of trees and rocks to hold on to.

"Have you had enough yet?" Ted asks as we reach the halfway point.

"Enough?"

"Of all this hiking around."

"Not at all. I could get used to this."

"It's addictive. I couldn't do what you do, sit in front of a computer all day."

"I'm not sure how much I can do of that either."

"The Forest Service could always use you," Ted says.

"I'll keep that in mind," I say, climbing down to the rocky shore of the river.

Recreational mining and panning have been commonplace in the rivers of Oregon going back to the middle of the nineteenth century. Millions of years of water cutting through the mountains, eroding the soil and splitting the rock, have made the area ripe for resource extraction. In the summer, these riverbanks will be occupied by visitors panning for gold, some travelling from out of state hoping to make a buck. In the Wild West days, when most people couldn't even pronounce the word *regulation*, miners dynamited the rocks alongside the river and dug long tunnels into the rock. Now the Bureau of Land Management cracks down on anything more elaborate than simple panning, and even that is prohibited while the salmon are spawning.

"But seriously," Ted says. "Are you considering a career change?"

We walk against the current, scanning the bank and the hill for the entrance of a long-abandoned mine.

"I've received an offer," I say, "for the website."

"A good one?"

"A great one," I say, "if you're talking about money."

"What does Saad think?"

"I haven't told him yet."

Ted pauses, turns at the waist and looks at me. He raises his eyebrow. "So, I'm your confidant now?"

"Shut up."

"Your bosom friend?"

"There's the mine," I say.

About fifteen feet up from the river, the adit sticks out against the wall of rock surrounding it.

"Ladies first," he says, bowing and making a sweeping gesture.

"Scared?" I ask.

Ted fakes a shiver. We click our flashlights on and scan around the adit. Ted raises his light high, pointing it over my shoulder.

"Be careful," he says, sincerely.

The earthen floor of the mine looks like it's been swept out. The pristine lines in the dirt, like those of Buddhist rock gardens in miniature, are easily disturbed and not likely to stay pristine very long. The walls have faint marks like someone has run a paint-brush over them. There is little else to see. It's clear that someone has been in here within the last few days.

"Anything?" Ted calls out from the opening.

"Definitely something," I say, "but I can't be sure what."

"It's getting dark," he says. "We'll have to hurry if you want to check that second mine before the sun's down completely."

"Just another few seconds," I say, as I take out my phone hoping to snap a few pictures.

"Shit!" Ted yells, and his light disappears.

"Ted?" I call out. "Ted!"

It's difficult to turn in the tight passage with my backpack on, difficult to even move. I'm the proverbial fish in a barrel right now. There's one exit, which is on a steep incline. I can't know if Ted fell because the ground gave way, or if he was attacked by God-knows-what, but whatever happened to him can almost certainly happen to me when I try getting out.

I peel out of the mine, quickly rolling against the wall to the right of the opening. At the foot of the hill is Ted's flashlight, shining against a small sumac and casting a shadow across the ground.

The blade is out so fast on the folding knife in my pocket I don't even know I did it.

All I hear is the sound of the river rushing and my own breathing.

"Ted," I say again, shining my beam concentrically from where I stand, reaching farther and farther out into the dusk.

"Here," he says from halfway down the hill. He's breathing heavily.

I slide down to his level and see he's clutching his chest.

"Are you all right?"

"I'll be all right," he says, and nods at the knife in my hand. "Won't be needing any field surgery."

Embarrassed, I fold the blade inward and shove the knife as deep down into my pocket as possible. "What happened?"

"I … I don't know," he says, still catching his breath.

Ted won't look at me. His gaze rests just past me, his head right back against the incline. He turns over before I can finish checking him for wounds, then stops squirming and lets out a sigh of relief. Everything goes quiet again. Then he looks up at me with his eyes impossibly blue, innocent like a child's, with a sincerity that just burns away doubt.

"I just saw fucking Bigfoot."

TWELVE

In its way, Bigfoot is like the vast number of mystical experiences, occult happenings, extra-sensory perceptions that have been recorded throughout man's history. The scientist cannot capture such experiences in formaldehyde nor record their existence with the electroencephalograph. Perhaps they don't exist but it is quite an ego experience to dismiss 5,000 years of recorded history as just so much delusion and wish fulfillment.

— *California Daily News*, June 25, 1970

THE MOUNTAIN IS NOTHING BUT A SILHOUETTE against the purple light of dusk. Clouds like waves reach and ripple across the sky. A passenger jet cuts diagonally across them. A cool breeze blows from the east, carrying the scent of Ted's aftershave toward me. I don't know the brand, but I imagine the ads for it feature a cowboy with a five o'clock shadow.

He's not saying anything more. Ever since he "saw Bigfoot," he's clammed up, wandering in a daze somewhere between shock and awe. We arrive at his truck and he freezes, stares at his silhouette in the driver's side window. He reaches for the door handle, then draws back again, turns and looks at me with frustration in his eyes. A crunching sound from the woods distracts him. His eyes dart along the treeline. It's almost night, only the closest trees are definable, the rest blend into shadow, a dark purple wall.

"Did I really see it?" he asks. "Or am I just losing it?"

"Tell me what you saw."

"Up the hill, standing over the opening of the mine. A big, shaggy man. Had to be a man, standing upright, bent over and looking at me. But long, dark hair. No clothes or anything. I was pulling out to make room for you, and I looked up and he was just there, watching me. I was so startled I fell back and rolled down the hill. Got the wind knocked out of me."

"What did it look like? Could you see its face?"

"I couldn't make out its face, or even its head, really. It was so shaggy that the head blended into the neck and shoulders. It disappeared so fast."

"Do you want me to drive?"

"No, I can … I'm okay to … sure." Ted puts the keys in the lock, then just leaves them there and walks around to the passenger side of the truck. "You can't tell anyone about this," he says. "Not even Saad."

"You can trust Saad."

"That's not the point," he says. "I don't need him looking at me funny."

"He won't."

"I just can't fucking believe this."

We skip the ranger station. Ted directs me down a back road between the park and town, to a small, single-storey cabin tucked among trees with a patch of gravel out front barely big enough to fit Ted's truck. I put the truck in park and we sit there. Ted doesn't speak. I take the keys out of the ignition and lean back in the driver's seat.

"I need a beer," he says, and gets out of the truck.

I get out, too, but I don't follow, choosing instead to lean against the door of the truck. I watch the lights flick on in the cabin through the windows. Watch him take a beer from the fridge and come over to the window, pointing at it.

"No thanks," I say, and shake my head for good measure.

He comes outside and sits on the tiny porch, pressing himself against the faux log cabin vinyl siding. With his elbows on his knees, he folds himself inward to make space for me. I sit down and text Saad the directions to Ted's cabin, then watch Ted drink his beer.

·   ●   ·

A car comes down the street slowly. It's got to be Saad, trying to find the place. I stand up and wave once I'm sure it's the rental car. Ted stays sitting on the porch, drinking his beer and staring out across the road at the patch of evergreen trees that are practically black without the sun. I wonder what he is seeing in that inkblot of branches moving in the wind.

"Hi, guys," Saad says. "Any luck with your search?"

I hesitate. "Well —"

"I saw Bigfoot," Ted says. "Deal with it."

THIRTEEN

A man-animal, according to a Southern
Pacific employee named Gary Joanis,
picked up a deer he had shot and fled with
the corpse into the tall timber.

— *San Francisco Chronicle*,
December 6, 1965

NIGHT HASN'T QUITE FALLEN AS WE FOLLOW
the lonely country roads back to the highway. The
headlights reflect off road signs and the occasional
moth. White cars stick out at a distance; their black
bumpers and tires are practically invisible, like the
frames are just floating over the asphalt. The woods
on either side of us are all shadows now, amorphous
except for the tops of the trees.

"What did Ted see?" Saad asks for the third time.

"A big, shaggy, upright-standing creature."

"And you didn't see it?"

"No."

"You didn't hear it?"

"No," I say. "And I didn't smell it."

"Okay?" Saad says. I can feel him peering at me.

"One part of the Bigfoot phenomenon, or the legend, is that the creature emits a strong odour, like a skunk. But I didn't smell anything like that either today or last night."

"Perhaps we can write off that element of the legend."

"We can write off everything until we have a specimen."

"This changes things, though, doesn't it?" Saad asks.

"How?"

"This time, the eyewitness is a forest ranger, an ex-soldier. Ted's not likely to mistake a bear for Bigfoot, is he? He's the most reliable witness we have."

Saad's certainty, on top of Ted's, leaves a bad taste in my mouth. I've been accused of being a contrarian, but I have a feeling in my stomach that this is all too easy. It took my dad years of trying, of bringing all his skills as a hunter and a soldier to bear, before he captured Bigfoot on tape. Whereas, since we got to Roanoke Ridge, there hasn't just been one sighting — there's been at least three. We must have set a world record for sightings in a three-day period.

Sure, the presence of a large search party and hordes of Bigfoot enthusiasts increases the chance of an encounter tenfold. I mean, the search for Professor Sorel has inadvertently become the largest Bigfoot hunt in history.

But sometimes a coincidence is just too much.

We get back to the motel, to the one remaining parking space. Music filters out softly through an open window. There is the sound of laughter, of glasses clinking. The breeze carries with it the thick, root-cellar smell of marijuana.

Our room is pitch black. Saad opens the door, hits the light switch, and freezes. I look in past him.

The VHS tapes from Driver's hideout are gone. Nothing else seems to be missing.

"I locked the door. The door was locked," Saad says, to avoid any blame.

"Let's check the bathroom."

There's a small frosted window in there that opens up onto the forest behind the motel, with a frame just wide enough to climb through. When we look inside, we see some mud on the toilet tank and on the lid, where someone used it as a stepladder. The water bottle Saad uses as a lota has been knocked over and spilled across the tiles.

"Why not take the laptop? Or the A/V equipment we borrowed?" Saad asks.

"Both good questions," I say, scanning the floor for any other traces. "Whoever did this doesn't want us trying to track them down or report it to the sheriff. If they'd taken our stuff we might decide it's worth swearing out a complaint, even though we obtained those tapes illegally. If all that is missing are things that didn't belong to us in the first place, that we have no right to, we're not likely to report it."

Saad, scratching his forearm, looks around the room as though he could have simply just misplaced the tapes. "Who would want to steal these videos?" he asks after a long silence.

"No idea," I say. "But, as far as I know, the sheriff's been the only one other than us who's been trying to find out where Driver's been hanging his figurative hat."

FOURTEEN

The recent glimpses of that strange and prehistoric looking creature, called Sasquatch, tend to confirm the belief that the missing link is still living!

— Ioganes Johnson, *Stag*, 1956

SAAD SITS IN THE ARMCHAIR, COMFORTER laid over his legs, watching a movie on his laptop. I can see the rapidly changing reflection in his glasses. A mixture of uneasiness and self-blame are keeping him up. He looks at me to see if I'm asleep.

I'm uneasy, too, but I know that no blame falls on either of us.

He quickly glances at the door, then gets up to check and re-check that it is bolted and that the chain is across. He even looks into the bathroom to make sure no marauders are climbing in through the window.

I don't remember falling asleep, but I wake as the light of dawn pours through the gaps in the curtains. Saad is in his bed, the covers over his head, one pillow having fallen to the floor. The parking lot is already buzzing with activity. The Bigfoot Festival has officially begun.

The Roanoke Valley Bigfoot Festival can be divided in two parts. One half is for the serious squatcher. The other half is for everybody else: every warm-blooded American who loves barbecues, three-legged races, tossing horseshoes, and the Little Miss Bigfoot Pageant. There's even a Bigfoot Demolition Derby, at the gravel pit just down the highway. And that's all on Saturday. On Sunday, the Lutheran church offers a pancake breakfast followed by Sasquatch Sunday Service. Then comes the Bigfoot Parade, the climax of the festival, followed by a cookout in Rotary Park, a belly-busting denouement for the whole family.

For the squatchers, the word *conference* is bandied about. The language they use is far more academic and professional: there are *talks*, *lectures*, and *discussions*, not to mention the odd screening of a new documentary. Aside from the outdoor lecture series taking place in Rotary Park this afternoon, most of the squatchers' meetings are in the Rotary Club itself, in the Bigfoot Museum, and in the basement of the Lutheran church. The indoor settings seem antithetical for those serious about finding an elusive beast, but I guess it helps them take themselves seriously among all the rubber-faced Bigfoot costumes and children with face paint and balloon animals.

Outside my window, a minivan fills with young women being chauffeured to the Miss Bigfoot Pageant. This is not to be confused with the Little Miss Bigfoot Pageant, for contestants ten and under. The Miss Bigfoot Pageant provides the opportunity for women in their late teens and early twenties to parade around in bikinis, perform absurd dance numbers, and display other talents for an audience of sweat-basted roughnecks who whistle because they can't clap loudly while holding a plastic cup filled with beer.

The last of the girls, a brunette with a pixie cut, looks right at me as she slides the door of the van shut, before it reverses and turns out of the motel parking lot, Lynyrd Skynyrd playing loudly.

Saad is dressed and ready. We're both starving.

Shirley's Bigfoot Diner is packed. The entire town's here. Had Ted not arrived early and waited in line, there's no way we'd get a table until after the morning rush.

Andrew Price, the comic book artist, lines up behind us, silently.

"We have room for one more," I say to him. "No pressure, though."

He shrugs his shoulders and follows, knapsack hanging from one shoulder. Beneath his baggy black hoodie are a bony frame, hunched shoulders, a pair of headphones around his neck, and what I imagine to be pale, beluga-like skin.

Ted takes Andrew in, head to toe, wearing a *can I help you* expression on his face. Andrew's look is that of a man who drinks by campfires and leaves his empty beer cans lying there, which is probably why Ted is suspicious of him.

"This is Andrew," I say to Ted. "He's an artist."

"And a writer," Andrew adds.

"Ted here is a forest ranger."

"Nice to meet you," Ted says.

Andrew sits down and hides himself in the menu. Ted looks at me with a hint of annoyance, and doesn't stop until I meet his gaze and hold it a while. Saad watches the staring contest from the sidelines.

"I was hoping we could discuss that encounter in the woods," Ted says.

"Me, too," I say.

"Privately."

"I wouldn't worry about it."

"Holy shit," Andrew says from behind the menu. "You saw Bigfoot, didn't you?"

All three of us turn toward Andrew.

"I don't know what I saw," Ted says. "Don't tell anybody that I said I saw Bigfoot, that's not true."

"Tell me what you saw, then. Describe it to me," Andrew says, taking a sketch pad out of his bag with Christmas-morning eagerness and laying it down on the table.

Ted leans in, his elbows on the table. "It was shaped like a man, but shaggier," he whispers. "Really shaggy, like an Afghan hound. It was big. It had black eyes with a sort of sheen to them, like crude oil. There was nothing apelike about its face."

Andrew starts with a crude, humanoid outline and adds detail from there. Like a forensic sketch artist, he draws a composite from Ted's description, turning his pad upside down so Ted can see it and correct details as he goes.

"He was leaner, not so top heavy. Yeah, that's about the length of the fur. No, the arms were longer, but not long enough to walk with, like a gorilla's."

As Andrew draws, we order our food and it arrives, steaming. We all dig in, except for him. He is possessed by whatever fuels him; Ted's voice the only one he hears. Finally, he lifts his pencil from the sketch pad and stares down at the page. He furrows his brow and scratches the bottom of his chin with the back of his pencil.

"Looks like Man-Thing," he says, then turns to me. "Doesn't it look like Man-Thing?"

I wrack my brain, trying to remember what Man-Thing is.

He slides the pad across the table to me, avoiding the plates and cutlery. I turn the pad around and look at the sketch. The creature is a hybrid of a scarecrow and the sludge of algae and dead grass that collects on the surface of a pond. Immediately I see it in my mind's eye, crawling out of a bayou and slowly marching toward a Hollywood scream queen with its arms held high and menacing. The image jogs my memory: the Man-Thing Andrew's referring to is the Marvel Comics version of the much better known

Swamp Thing. I remember not being able to tell the difference between them.

"You're right," I say. "It does look like Man-Thing."

Saad picks up the pad and squints. He's not wearing his glasses. Ted leans in and says, "That's him, all right."

"Cool," Andrew says.

Ours becomes the quietest, most reticent table in the diner. Even the waitress is taken aback by the solemnity of the three young men sitting around me.

"Are you up to this?" I ask Ted.

"Yeah, oh yeah. I'm ready."

"Ready for what?" Andrew asks.

We set out into the woods for what may be the last time. The sun is high above us, permeating the naked branches with ease. I feel like I should have worn sunscreen on the back of my neck — part of me craves the sun, though, like a lizard would. The mountain looms behind us, like a parent watching over us as we set out deep into the wilderness. There's an odd feeling in my stomach. Not because I fear we might be rent limb from limb by Bigfoot — it's because even though the forest in front of me seems limitless, it feels like we're running out of mystery.

Ted's different this time out. He's quiet now, unsure. Saad is still Saad, bringing up the rear, weighed down with the curiosity of a tourist. He can't help it, maybe he doesn't even realize when he pauses at the base of a

Pacific silver fir or leans over a bearberry bush, known locally as a kinnikinnick. We hear what sounds like a cry, and Saad is shocked awake. It sounds like a child, but I recognize the sound. So does Ted.

"Nuthatch," I say.

After an hour and a half on foot, we come to the first of the three abandoned mines I want to search. From the trail the mine is invisible, like something out of a fairy tale — we would've passed it if Ted's GPS hadn't pinged to alert us that we'd arrived. Because the Pacific Northwest's winters differ from those of most of the continent, even in the early spring there is a lot of green between the pine trees and the moss that grows on every rock and rotting log. We have to peel back this veil to find the mine, and even then, we don't see its gaping mouth until we are less than ten feet from it.

The adit of the mine is tucked between two walls of solid rock. A dead stump sits on top, its dry and life-less roots hanging down over the entrance. The timber that once acted as a lintel for the adit has fallen down on one side, creating a diagonal barrier. One expects to see a spider's web sealing the gaps on either side of the timber, but the whole area is clear.

The three of us approach it more like a SWAT team now. The *wik-wik-wik* of a pileated woodpecker echoes through the forest and startles us all. There's a tension in us that just wasn't there before. Ted surveys the area around the mine before we get close. And this time, Saad insists on clearing the entrance of any immediate danger before I crawl inside. He shines his light into the black mouth of the mine before stepping aside. "Maybe I should go in," he says.

"I can do it," Ted says.

"I know you can, but I will, if you two don't mind," I say.

Ted had brought two mining helmets from the ranger station. He hands one to me now. I turn the headlamp on and then fasten the strap under my chin, before approaching the entrance. Gently, I push the fallen timber to the side. It gives a bit, so I lean in close to move it. That's when I see some burlap fibres on the edge of the wood, as well as blades of dry grass.

"Check this out," I say, pointing to the fibres.

Inside, invertebrates scurry out of my headlamp's glow. The opening of the mine is dry, the timber beams show few signs of rot. There are no tracks for mine-carts, but two ruts are visible in the dirt. It looks like the miners used a wheelbarrow to cart ore out. Just like the mine from yesterday, the floor and walls look like they were swept out with a broom.

I snap and place some glow sticks in the walls — cracks in the strata provide the perfect crevices — and the mine slowly begins to fill with an amber aura. Ted comes in behind me. Saad remains outside, sticking tightly to the rock wall next to the adit, and I feel better knowing we have the entrance covered.

"According to our records, this mine's been here close to a hundred years," Ted says.

Large spiders look down on us from the ceiling, their backs covered in eyes.

"That's disgusting," I say, as the beam from my headlamp falls upon a particularly large, particularly ugly orange spider with long, crablike legs more than two inches across.

"*Trogloraptor*," Ted says. "It means 'cave robber.' This species was only named in 2012. I've never seen one before in person. Oregon is home to over five hundred species of spiders."

"Usually I'm not grossed out by spiders, but that one is …"

"Butt-ugly, I know."

It starts moving along the ceiling, not liking the attention it's receiving, or all the light, and I have an impulse to flatten it, to kill it just for making me uncomfortable. Behaviour my dad wouldn't stand for.

Deeper in, the rock walls are cool and damp, though the floor of the mine remains dry, made up of a fine sand, almost like ash that has been ground under a boot. Ted and I walk slowly, taking small steps with extreme care. It makes our journey feel longer. As the tunnel curves around jagged rock edges, we lose the light flowing through the adit. The spiders disappear. All the invertebrates are gone now. There is nothing living at the back of the mine except Ted and I. It feels like we're lost.

"Are you guys okay?" Saad yells, his voice sounding as if he's speaking through a tube.

"A-okay," Ted says.

We come to the end of the tunnel. It's a wall of solid rock, a coolness radiating from it like an open refrigerator. The dirt on the floor here has been disturbed, as if someone had set up a sleeping bag and spent the night.

"See that?" I say.

"Looks like we had a camper," Ted says. "This is the last place you'd stay if you wanted to be found."

Kneeling down, I shine my flashlight against the rocks to the left of the disturbed sand. There's an oil slick on the wall, a paint-like smear that resembles Chinese calligraphy. I take a latex glove out of my pocket, put it on, and wipe the smear. My latex-wrapped fingertips are red under the beam of my flashlight.

"Blood," I say. "Fresh blood." I shine the flashlight around the rest of the cave. "There's more."

In the opposite corner, a grey igneous rock sparkles when I shine my light on it. The ash-like sand has been swept up against it, carefully, to hide that it has been moved. I stick my fingers between the rock and the wall and pry it away. In a pit behind the rock I find some wrappers for a gauze pack, medical tape, and a small bottle of rubbing alcohol. Using my knife to move the refuse around, I also find an MRE wrapper. Chicken teriyaki.

"What is it?" Ted asks.

"The absolute last thing I wanted to find," I say.

FIFTEEN

Patterson said he felt the search for Bigfoot
is drawing to a close. "We know enough
about Bigfoot's habit and habitats that
we should be able to soon lure one into
a position where we can capture it,"
Patterson declared.

— *Oregon Journal*, March 11, 1969

I'M DREAMING I'M ON A FERRY CROSSING A
rough sea, saltwater spraying over the sides of the boat,
when Saad nudges me awake from the driver's seat.

We're parked in the parking lot of the Golden Eagle
Motel. The whole place is empty now. Everybody else
has already made their way to the centre of town for
the Bigfoot Parade. The floats are gathered at the
empty lot just north of here, forming a line and slowly
turning onto the highway.

Saad points out the window. A Bigfoot is creeping
around the side of the motel, before taking a big step up

onto the porch. Its reddish-brown fur turns a shade darker beneath the awning and stands in stark contrast to the white-painted boards that make up the outer wall. This is not the creature from Andrew's sketch. When it looks around, Saad and I sit low in our seats, concealed by the dirty windshield. The creature skulks over to the door of Barbara Sorel's room, reaching under the white T-shirt it's wearing to produce a key. It quickly disappears inside.

Thankfully, Barbara is not there. She is where she's been the last three days — sitting anxiously in the ranger station, awaiting word about her husband. Seeing a hairy ape-man walk into her motel room would be a devastating blow to her already-fragile heart.

"This is going to hurt her badly," Saad says. "There may be no coming back from it."

"I know," I say. "Why did it have to be me?"

"It could only be you," Saad says.

Minutes later the Bigfoot exits the motel, pulling the door closed and locking it. One thing is clear, as Bigfoot walks past the motel room doors and the humming Pepsi machine: it's missing the trademark arm swing made famous in Frame 352 of the PG film. In fact, its left arm isn't moving at all, just hanging by its side like an empty sleeve.

"He had to come back sooner or later," I say. "Now is the best time."

The Sasquatch walks to the end of the motel driveway. Saad and I get out of our rental car and follow on foot. I wear a baseball cap and sunglasses. It should be enough of a disguise. I look like everybody else waiting to watch the parade.

It's a beautiful day for the festival — the hottest April day in Roanoke Valley history, beating the previous record, set in 1962, by seven degrees. Spectators approach the road in T-shirts and shorts. The sheriff's department has closed off one lane of traffic with orange road pylons. More and more, a crowd gathers, pressing in on the asphalt that begins to cook in the sun.

A father and his two sons stand near the gravel shoulder of the highway, staring up the road that winds around outcrops of rocks and windblown pine trees, waiting for the parade to start. One of the little boys turns and sees the Sasquatch, leans back into the safety of his father's legs. The father says something to the Sasquatch, who stops and poses with the son while the father takes a picture with his phone. After, as Sasquatch backs away, it bangs into a telephone pole and claps its hand over its shoulder. Its apelike face, moulded into permanent shock and disgust, turns and looks at the pole as though it hurt it on purpose.

Before turning around again, the eyeholes beneath its pronounced brow ridge sweep over me and lock in on my face. Does it recognize me? I behave casually. I don't slow down. Saad follows my cue, acting as though we are tourists.

The first vehicles in the parade turn around the bend. Horns honk and pale arms wave in the golden sun. First up are two deputies on motorcycles, acting like a presidential motorcade. In the convertible behind them, Miss Bigfoot 2016 sits up on the back seat, a bouquet of flowers in one arm, a sash across her shoulder.

The Bigfoot is walking a little faster now. It looks agitated. Is it the injury? Or is there a clock counting down that I don't know about? It glances over its shoulder again, the corner of its rubber scowl visible over tufts of fake fur. The Sasquatch looks straight ahead, the mountains off in the distance. Then it bolts.

For the first time in my life, I see a wounded Sasquatch running straight into a crowd of people holding cotton candy. It has a head start, but it's hurt, cradling its left arm. Saad is behind me, trying to capture the whole thing on his cellphone camera. I know, I just know that the video will be one long blur and I may as well be chasing Santa Claus. It'll never hold up, definitely not in a court of law. Saad breathes heavily, his feet slapping on the concrete. I feel better knowing he's here.

The air is hot and thick with the smell of burgers and hot dogs cooking on a half-dozen barbecues. The Sasquatch turns a corner and almost knocks over a little boy with a snow cone in one hand and his mother's hand in the other. I gain on the furry ape-man as it runs right across the main street, between floats and into a curious crowd. I run in front of an old black convertible with a trio of silver-haired women from the Ladies' Auxiliary who are throwing packets of candy into the crowd. Behind the wheel is a fat old guy with dark Elvis-style sunglasses. He honks at me, but I keep running.

There is only one place the Bigfoot could be going, the one place where it could park a car between the motel and the mountain that wouldn't be swallowed up by the parade. It runs behind the drugstore, down a side street that slopes down into a parking lot. There's no question of primate locomotion here, bipedalism versus brachiation versus quadrapedalism. It's just running, running for its life. It's opened up its wound — I can see the blood soaking into the Pace Hardware Store T-shirt overtop the red-brown fur. The Sasquatch runs between parked cars and fiddles around its waistline like it's trying to find car keys.

"Stop!" I yell.

It's a beautiful day; a wall of evergreen trees rises up behind the Sasquatch, just across the river. This whole town is like paradise, nestled among mountains and river valleys.

Behind the Sasquatch is a short concrete wall built at the edge of the parking lot, then the steep drop to the Klamath River, the midday sun glinting off the peaks of the water. Most apes aren't very good swimmers; they aren't very buoyant, and this one is badly injured. The only way out is the road. Saad catches up to me, out of breath, and we stand together in the mouth of the driveway. There's no driving out of here without driving through us. Even the legendary Sasquatch isn't stupid enough to commit vehicular manslaughter in broad daylight, hundreds of witnesses fifty feet away. Or at least I hope it isn't.

"Professor," I say. "Please."

Ted pulls up in his truck, parking it across the driveway, forming a backstop.

The Sasquatch cradles his wounded arm, bulging out from under his costume, and leans against an old rust-bottomed Caprice, looking at something off in the distance. He's tired, he's wounded, and he's old.

When I was younger, Professor Sorel's obsessive tendencies, his eccentricities, his desire to take on all of academia, seemed noble and romantic. Young adults trying to navigate the adult world often seem to conflate mental illness and genius. We love the little guy fighting against the establishment. But now I'm starting to see the cracks in the foundation.

"I've been a real fool," he says, pulling the mask off with his good hand.

"Happens to the best of us," I say.

The sheriff comes running around the pharmacy with one hand on his holster and the other one pressing his hat to his head. The tough Sam-Elliot demeanour that he presented all this time is replaced with the body language of Don Knotts. His age is showing, his frailty. I can see why he is so afraid of being replaced.

"It was an accident," Professor Sorel says. "I want you to know that, I need you to know that."

He drops the mask, which pancakes on the chewed-up concrete of the parking lot.

"I know that," I tell him.

"Barb is gonna be ticked off," he says.

The sheriff approaches Professor Sorel slowly, as though he's a wounded animal, and tries to cuff him. As I thought, and as Sheriff Watkins learns the hard way, the left arm is an empty sleeve. Watkins then leads Professor Sorel over to the ambulance that has pulled up, where Moira waits to look at his wounded arm.

Professor Sorrel looks at me again, this time with only a passing recognition, as he is walked by the lawman. There is no rage, no look of incredulity or betrayal. His brown eyes are sad; his head hangs like that of a dog that chewed up its master's slippers.

"That is not the Bigfoot I saw in the woods," Ted says through his open window.

"I know. What you saw was Professor Sorel in a ghillie suit."

Ted tilts his head back, rolling his eyes. "Of course."

"How did you know where to find us?" I ask.

"Turns out running through the middle of a parade causes a scene," Ted says, smiling.

"What's a ghillie suit?" Saad asks.

"It's a wearable camouflage worn by hunters or snipers. It's often made of army fatigues with a burlap mesh overtop and leaves and grass woven into it. Ghillie suits are actually called yowie suits in Australia, due to their resemblance to the fabled ape-man of the outback. I wouldn't be surprised if that's what gave Professor Sorel the idea."

"Why was he hiding?" Saad asks.

I don't know how to answer him, until I remember the story of one of the first real squatchers. A Swiss-Canadian man named René Dahinden lost his wife and children through his relentless quest for Bigfoot — not to mention over forty years of his life. And he still never found the creature. Maybe Professor Sorel saw that his time was running out. Maybe he launched a Hail Mary, in the one place he was sure Bigfoot could be found.

"He hid so that we would look for him," I finally say. "And so we'd bring in a hundred volunteers and search and rescue helicopters with infrared cameras."

"To make up for the drones he was unable to afford," Saad says. "More people to potentially spot Bigfoot."

Ted asks, "What do you think happened to Rick Driver?"

"Rick Driver found out where my father's footage was shot. My guess is he, too, was curious whether a Sasquatch lived up on that mountain. Oddly enough, many hoaxers are themselves true believers. But his being around got in the professor's way, so the professor tried driving him off — doing so in accordance to the Sasquatch legend."

"By throwing rocks at him," Saad says.

"Yes, like the Ape Canyon incident."

Ted wipes the corners of his mouth with his thumb and forefinger, then looks off at the water of the Klamath. "So a man died over a stupid prank? All to prove that an ape lives in the woods of Oregon."

"After realizing Driver was dead, Professor Sorel kept up the act, even calling back to those squatchers on the mountain. Everyone started to believe. Even you, Ted."

"I —"

"You saw what you were expecting to see. All the hype, the hysteria, it got to you. It got to a lot of people. There's no shame in that. Happens all the time."

Ted looks at me and smiles, then turns to Saad.

"Don't look at me," Saad says. "I grew up in a household where djinn were real and Gog and Magog were real monsters constantly chewing their way out of a mountain. I'm in no position to judge you."

They exchange a nod. A bromance is budding between them.

Professor Sorel sits on the bumper of the ambulance, its open doors like a pair of butterfly wings, as Barbara Sorel is escorted through the gawking crowd by the female deputy whose name I still don't know. She walks like she has no control over her own body without the deputy guiding her. Barbara's eyes glisten as they sweep over the gathering crowd then stare blankly at her husband. Professor Sorel doesn't look at her, or over at me anymore, not once. Instead he seems to count the cracks in the cement, tracing their paths with his eyes.

"Are you okay?" Saad asks me.

"To be honest, I have no idea what I'm feeling," I say. "If I'm feeling anything at all."

I want to go to Barbara, to hold her and console her. She needs a friend. But, what if she blames me for getting her husband arrested?

"You know this isn't your fault, right? None of this is your fault," Saad says.

"We have to go back to that house."

"What? Why?"

"I have to know if the film my father shot was a hoax perpetrated by him and Rick Driver."

"Does that matter right now?"

"It does, Saad. I need to know if what happened here today is really my dad's fault."

SIXTEEN

What does the evidence tell us, where does
it lead us, and is there something behind
this phenomenon in western North
America?

— Dr. Jeff Meldrum, *Author Interviews*,
NPR, November 10, 2006

THE JOHANSSON HOUSE IS INVISIBLE IN THE
starlight, a charcoal smudge in a sea of shadows. Saad
shines his flashlight on the broken porch steps while I
climb up. I return the favour. The boards creak as we
walk, the door squeals on its hinges.

"This is like *Evil Dead*," Saad says.

"That's the last thing I want to hear."

Entering the house, I hold my empty hand up defen-
sively as my beam zeroes in on the light switch. When
I flick it, nothing happens. It is the same with the light
switch in the dining room, and the cord dangling from
the light in the stairwell.

"Let's get to the attic, then get out of here," Saad says.

"I couldn't agree more," I say.

He shines his beam on the wood planks that make up each step to the second floor, and I shine mine straight ahead, as we climb to the upstairs hallway. There's a window at the end, and I thank the god I'm not sure I believe in that there's no silhouette there, lurking, waiting to lunge at us. I pull the cord hanging from the ceiling and get the ladder down, but Saad insists on going first, like he has something to prove.

The attic seems bigger in the darkness, each corner composed of limitless shadow. The only depth, the only dimension that I can measure is what is directly within the glow of my flashlight. We both move slowly, knowing that we're in a minefield of tripping hazards.

"Where do we even start?" I say, shining my beam over every box in my orbit.

"I'll check the trunk," Saad says.

"Good idea." As he does, I crouch down and begin to read the sides of the boxes. Sliding boxes left and right, I survey half the contents of the attic without finding anything useful until, against the sloping roof, tucked tight into the rafter, I find a cardboard box labelled, in faded marker, NATE'S CRAP. *Nate* for Nate Reagan. My dad.

"Look at this," Saad says.

I shine my flashlight over in his direction. Saad, with his flashlight tucked under his left arm, is holding up a costume. Not the gorilla costume from the first time we were here — that hangs over the side of the trunk, its mask on the floor, empty eyeholes staring at me. The costume Saad holds is almost like a rain slicker made of fur. There are little elastic loops, one on each limb, to hold it in place. The suit is small, a good fit for a child.

"What do you think it is?" Saad asks.

"I have an idea, but I don't want to say."

Something bangs outside, harder and closer than a car door slamming. I shut my light off and Saad follows suit. He turns and looks out the window.

"Do you see anything?" I whisper.

"Nothing."

I crawl over to the ladder and lean down through the opening. The front door squeals again, then I hear soft footprints on the old floorboards. Taking my cellphone out of my pocket, I call Ted.

"Yello?" he says, his voice audible only through the phone and not, as I had hoped, from downstairs.

"Where are you?" I whisper.

"I'm at the Paul."

"Shit."

"Why? What's up?"

"We're at Driver's house, in the attic. Someone just came in."

"Shit," he says. "I'm on my way."

"Call me when you're here."

I switch my phone to vibrate and slip it back in my pocket. Then, reaching down, I grab as low a rung as I can reach and pull. The telescoping ladder folds back within itself. I pull it shut and give it an extra tug to be sure. Saad puts the fur suit down and gingerly walks back toward me.

"What are we going to do?" he whispers.

"I don't know what we can do. Our rental car is parked out front. It's obvious that we're in here."

"What if it's the same person who broke in to our motel room?"

"Then we hide out for as long as possible, and if someone tries to climb up here we rain boxes down on them like Donkey Kong."

I crawl across the floor carefully, like it's an ice sheet that might crack, toward the box with my dad's name on it. Pulling open the cardboard flaps, I tense up a little at the sound they make as they scrape against each other. I rest my flashlight inside the box with the LEDs pointed toward the bottom, to contain the light, and turn it on. At the top of the box is an old flannel shirt. It still smells like my dad's aftershave. At least I think it does — I don't see how it can after all these years. Under the shirt is a pair of blue-and-yellow plastic Fisher Price binoculars. I used to take them on our camping trips; I was never sure what happened to them. I slip my hand to the bottom of the box and feel around the perimeter. Against the side of the box is a plastic square or rectangle. I lift it and hold it near the light. It's a tape, too small for VHS, more the kind of cassette that fits into an old Handycam. The label reads RR 05/10-93.

The cassette fits perfectly into my back pocket. I army crawl back to Saad, and we both stay still and listen as, beneath us, footsteps creep along slowly. They stop just under the door leading to the attic. My eyes have adjusted to the darkness, enough to see Saad looking back at me. I nod, because it seems like the only thing to do.

It's quiet below us for a while. There are no more footsteps, no voices. Part of me anticipates the ladder to be yanked down violently and for light to flood the attic — but there's nothing, until, finally, the floorboards creak again, the sound growing fainter as the person walks back toward the stairs. I can hear each thud as the person goes down the stairs to the main floor, then the squeal of the door opening and the slap of it closing. We wait, looking down at the floor as if we have X-ray vision, then back at each other. A wind kicks up outside, wheezes through the cracks around the window.

Saad and I are both startled by my phone vibrating. I pull it out and recognize Ted's number.

"I'm in the driveway," he says. "I don't see anyone."

"There's no electricity. Make sure you have your flashlight," I whisper.

"I'm covered. I brought the floodlight from my trunk."

"Be careful."

"I will," he says. "I'm at the front porch now. Still no sign of anyone."

"There might be someone else in the house," I say.

"I'm armed."

"You brought a gun?"

"Bear spray. More effective in a bear attack than a gun."

The door creaks open again.

"Better get off the phone," Ted says. "Just in case."

Saad looks at me, waiting for a cue. The house is quiet.

Ted's still not here. If I have to guess, I'd say it's seven seconds from the door to the stairs, four seconds to climb them, then another five to get to the ladder that leads to the attic. Even if you double that time to account for the darkness and the unfamiliarity, then double it again, Ted should be right below us. What's taking him so long?

I call his phone and hear, faintly, his ringtone: "Sweet Child O' Mine" by Guns N' Roses. It's far away, but I can't tell how far. I let it ring, and the song echoes through the hall.

If whoever we heard before is still down there, I can't let them have the tape. I take my shoe off, then my sock, and put the cassette in the sock. Then I crawl to the window. It's a long way down. I see an orange extension cord in the corner, and tie it to the sock. Then I lift the window up just enough to lower the sock and cord down to the ground.

Saad turns on his flashlight again and looks around for weapons. There is an ugly shadeless and bulbless lamp that is a good size for him. I pick up what looks like an old kerosene jug made out of tin. There isn't much else that would be of any use.

I call Ted again. More "Sweet Child O' Mine," all the way to Ted's voice mail.

If Ted's in trouble, we can't wait any longer. I lean on the ladder until the hatch opens and the ladder lowers to the floor, holding it all the way down so it won't make a loud thud, but every noise is like a gunshot in such a quiet place. I climb down first, before Saad can object.

We don't turn our lights on; we go by feel. My shoulder brushes against the wall as I slowly walk down the hallway. When we reach the stairs, we have no choice but to turn a flashlight on. We take each step together, him against the railing on my right, me against the wall.

At the bottom of the stairs we turn in opposite directions and shine our beams through the empty house, looking for any sign of Ted. My flashlight reflects off a dusty mirror and shines on some old cobalt-blue and amber bottles sitting in a row on the windowsill. I call Ted one more time and hear "Sweet Child O' Mine" from the next room.

The glow of an LCD screen lights up the kitchen floor. Next to the phone, on the curling linoleum floor, is Ted, eyes closed with a trickle of blood running down his forehead.

"Shut your lights off," a voice growls from the corner, behind the wood stove.

A floodlight, maybe Ted's, turns on and blinds us.

"Shut those lights off," he says again. "And put those antiques down."

Saad and I do as we're told, letting the lamp and the kerosene can fall to the floor. The figure of a man, barely visible in the backsplash of the floodlight, shifts slightly. There's a clicking sound, like the hammer being drawn back on a pistol. There's something in his hand, but I can't confirm it's a gun.

"Empty your pockets," he says.

Saad and I lay our flashlights on the kitchen table, followed by keys, wallets, phones, lip balm.

"Show me your beltlines," he says.

Saad and I lift our shirt fronts and the figure shines his flashlight on our bare stomachs.

"Now turn around. Pick up your things, then carry your friend out of here."

There's a smell in the air that I didn't notice until now. Gasoline. The man sets the floodlight on the table and takes a step back into the darkest corner. He pulls out a lighter. The clicks, the sparks, give it away before the flame. Saad grabs one of Ted's arms, I take the other, and we drag him toward the door.

The man holds the light far from his face, but it's clear he's wearing a ski mask. "Keep moving," he says. "Faster." When we get out on the porch, he tosses the lighter inside. Flames snake through the kitchen, into the dining room and den. The gossamer curtains turn orange in the glow, as the entire ground floor is quickly engulfed. The masked man passes us quickly, hopping down the broken staircase, onto the grass.

Saad hops down to the grass and opens his arms wide. "Hurry, slide Ted down to me," he says. Half rolling Ted, we get him down the steps and into Saad's arms. I jump down and we both pull him clear.

A car door slams somewhere in the distance. An engine starts.

"Look after him," I say to Saad.

Having left my flashlight inside, I use my phone's flashlight function to scour the grass near the attic window. When I see the orange of the extension cord, I follow it to my sock. I untie the sock as I walk, coming around the corner of the house to see that Ted is waking up.

"What happened?" he asks, dabbing his forehead with his fingertips and looking at the blood.

"You lost your bear spray," I say, pointing to the flames. I can feel the heat coming out of the house.

"Got more in the trunk," he says.

"We need to get Ted to a hospital," I tell Saad.

"I'm fine," Ted says.

"You need to have that looked at," I say.

"No doctors. I'll make the call."

Moira knocks quietly on our motel room door. She smiles without showing any teeth, bows her head, and walks right over to Ted, who sits in the powder-blue armchair against the west wall. He sucks his teeth as she cleans his wound with rubbing alcohol.

I sit on the edge of my bed, turning the cassette over and over in my hands. Headlights shine through the curtains and I glance up at the door to make sure it's locked and that the chain is across.

Saad sits down next to me. "What do you think is on the tape?" he asks quietly.

"I'm hoping I'm wrong, but I think it's evidence that the Roanoke Ridge film was a hoax. What else could it be?"

"You said the sheriff was trying hard to find Driver's residence? Do you think it's because he's after these videos?"

"Maybe. He's been tearing this town apart looking for Rick Driver's stuff. He knew Rick, he knew my father. Maybe he was in on the hoax," I say. "And he milked it for all it was worth, made a cottage industry out of Bigfoot around here. Keeping this town prosperous while presiding over it like a medieval lord."

"We have no proof," Saad says.

"What we need right now is a way to play this tape."

I take a business card off the table, where I tossed it the other day, and dial the number.

"Hello," Danny LeDoux answers.

"Hi, Danny. It's Laura Reagan."

"Hello, Laura. Is this call business or personal?"

"All business," I say. "Do you have any equipment that can read a Video8 cassette?"

"You know it."

"How soon can you get it here?"

"How soon can I get it there? Why would I want to do that?"

"We have some tape that I think would be as much worth your while as it is mine."

"I've heard that before." I can hear the suction of his lips parting into a smile.

"Hurry up and get here before something happens to it."

I hang up. Saad looks at me with raised eyebrows.

"He'll be here," I say.

"Don't worry about me," Ted says from his chair behind us. "I'm fine."

"Is he fine?" I ask Moira.

She shines a pocket flashlight into his eyes.

"No signs of a concussion," she says. "And he doesn't need stitches."

We sit in silence for a while, until it's broken by a gentle knocking. Parting the curtain, I see the NatureWorld van in the parking lot, its headlights still on and Chris behind the wheel. Danny stands at our door, adjusting his tie.

"Still got the tape?" he asks as I open the door.

"Yes."

I notice that his hands are empty.

"Where's the equipment?" I ask.

Danny turns and waves to Chris. The headlights go dark and the engine shuts off. Chris gets out and goes around the side of the van, opens the sliding door, and leans in.

"What's so special about this tape?" Danny asks.

"We're about to find out," I say. "We were almost killed getting a hold of it, so I hope there's something of value."

"What? Killed? You're going to have to explain that."

Chris comes between us cradling a camcorder in his arms, a bundle of cables hanging over his wrists. I lock the door behind him and put the chain across.

"Good thing I keep this guy around," Chris says, nodding at the camcorder. "This was my first camera starting out. I shot *Hauntings in the 'Hood* and

Psychic Pets with this bad boy. Lucky for you it's backward compatible."

Saad shifts the TV to the far left side of the dresser to make room for his laptop. Chris attaches all the cords to his camcorder, then connects them to the laptop before I hand him the cassette. It only takes a few minutes to bring this early nineties technology into the twenty-first century. Chris moves in close to the keyboard and Saad steps to the side.

Suddenly, the lights shut off, leaving the room awash in the blue glow of the monitor. We look around at each other and see only half faces and profiles. Nobody says a word.

Danny opens his mouth, then a car alarm sounds from the parking lot. I look through the curtains and see that the NatureWorld van's headlights are flashing.

"It's your van," I say.

"Chris," Danny says. "Check it out."

I unlock the door to let him outside. There are no lights, no electricity anywhere around the motel. The headlights of the van are all that hold back the rabid darkness of night. Other doors open and other motel patrons look around outside. Chris walks around the van, checks the doors, and then shrugs. He shuts the alarm off and comes back inside.

Closing the door behind him, I slide the chain across for what feels like the hundredth time, when a different alarm sounds. Saad beats me to the window and looks out, but I get there before he can tell me.

It's our vehicle this time. Saad shuts the alarm off remotely.

"It's safe to assume that somebody is messing with us," LeDoux says. "Let's watch this video while we can."

There's a knock at the door. Saad walks back over to the curtains.

"Be careful," I say, remembering the gun that was pointed at us an hour earlier.

"It's the sheriff," Saad says.

Watkins knocks again. "Laura," he calls through the door.

"Saad," I whisper. "You and Chris take the gear into the bathroom and copy it onto your hard drive."

When they go, Ted sits up straight and looks ready for action. Moira looks over at me like I'm in control of this situation. I wish that were true.

That's when I notice the glow of Saad's laptop screen leaking out from under the bathroom door. I take the miniature Maglite out of my bag and switch it to candle mode. Its soft glow barely makes up for that of the laptop, so LeDoux and Moira both turn the lights on their phones on and I use my other flashlight. Soon the room is lit almost as though the electricity was back on.

"Danny, please stand over by the bathroom door. We may need to stall the sheriff."

He moves into position with visible reluctance. I imagine it would be the same for any request I could make of him — he's not the type who likes listening to others.

I walk over to the door and open it, leaving the chain across. "Good evening, Sheriff."

"Evening, Laura," he says, examining the chain. "Can I come in?"

"What's this about?"

"For God's sake, Laura, you're not in any trouble. Can't we talk like two civilized people?"

I open the door and catch a look of surprise on the sheriff's face as he does a head count of the room. "Is everything all right?" he asks quietly.

"I'm still trying to figure that out."

"Ranger Cassavetes, Moira, Mr. LeDoux," he says, greeting everyone around the room in turn. "Clive the manager called to report the power outage and the alarms going off in the parking lot. I was just leaving the Paul so I thought I'd check up on the place."

"So why knock on my door?"

"Well, you seem to be at the centre of all the trouble lately."

"Can't argue with that, I suppose."

He looks over my shoulder at Ted, squinting to see his bandaged head wound.

"Ranger Cassavetes, what the hell happened to you?"

"I'm not entirely sure," Ted says.

"Okay, enough games, I expect you all to come clean with me now."

Sirens ring out from down the street. The red flashing lights of a fire engine light up the night and cast a red glow on the curtains.

The sheriff takes a step back out into the parking lot. "What the hell is going on now?"

The volunteer firefighters dismount off the truck and fan out. Clive the motel manager comes out to greet them. He shakes his head to whatever they ask him, pointing at several doors.

"All right, folks," a firefighter shouts. "Everybody out."

A second firefighter starts working his way door to door.

"You heard the man — out!" Sheriff Watkins says before walking toward the fire chief. Chris and Saad come out of the bathroom. Chris is holding the camcorder.

"Is the transfer complete?" I ask, whispering.

"No," Saad says.

"Let's just get that video copied," I say. "We'll worry about fire once we at least smell smoke."

"No thanks, missy," LeDoux says. "It's my ass if anything happens to my staff or equipment. Chris, move it onto the van."

A firefighter comes to the doorway. "What are you waiting for?"

As LeDoux and I stare each other down, Moira helps Ted up and walks him out. Then Saad passes between us, his head down.

LeDoux makes a sweeping gesture with his arm. "After you," he says to me.

"Please," the fire chief says. "Everybody move to the other side of the parking lot. We received a report of a fire on the premises."

As the other patrons of the Tall Pines Motel gather beneath the stars, hands in pockets or arms crossed, I focus on the camera Chris is holding. I can hear a late-night, conspiracy talk show host's favourite line repeat in my head: *I don't believe in coincidences*. Personally, I do believe in coincidences, but this all seems like too much.

The sheriff is going door to door with the fire chief, making a final sweep of the rooms while the firefighters investigate for signs of smoke or heat.

Clive walks over to us. "Sorry about all the ruckus, folks," he says. He's wearing a long overcoat like he's expecting rain, or is about to flash us. "At least it's a nice night. No rain, no wind. First good night for camping we've had this year."

Clive's wife, wrapped in a housecoat, stands away from us, watching her husband, giving off that vibe of wanting to be next to him — a sign that men are terrible at picking up on.

Now he enters the focal point of our semicircle, a forearm's length closer than what seems natural. He glances at the butterfly bandage on Ted's head but doesn't ask about it. Then he sidles up next to Chris and points up at the roof of the motel. "I don't see any smoke or anything, do you? You'd think you'd see something rising up over the roof by now."

As Clive works his way in between Chris and LeDoux, like the family dog, I notice there's something round and heavy in his pocket, something that causes his jacket to sway like a pendulum when it moves. I look from his coat pockets to the camcorder held at the same level.

"Chris, could you come here, please?" I say.

"What?"

"Could you come here, please," I say again.

He walks over, and Clive's eyes follow the camcorder.

"That's a neat old camcorder," Clive says. "Can I see it?"

"No!" I shout. "Chris, move!"

Clive makes a lunge for the camera, but Chris has good reflexes. Like a high-school football player, Chris curls his body over the camcorder and ploughs forward. Ted and Saad both reach for Clive. He shakes off their initial half-hearted grabs but succumbs to the second, more concerted attempts. Chris is now six feet away and swivels to face his assailant, cradling the camera like a protective mother. Ted and Saad let Clive go, but their bodies form a barrier between him and the camcorder.

"What the hell is going on here?" Sheriff Watkins says, hurrying across the parking lot.

"I just wanted to see their camcorder, Sheriff," Clive says. "I didn't know it'd be such a big deal."

"Laura?" the sheriff says, raising an eyebrow at me.

"He was trying to erase the tape in that camera," I say.

"What?" Clive says, aghast at the accusation.

"I bet there's a big magnet in his pocket, probably from a speaker or something. He's trying to demagnetize the videotape," I say.

Saad takes a step back from Clive and starts examining his clothing. I shine my flashlight on Clive's pocket, and he turns to avoid the beam.

"What videotape?" Sheriff Watkins asks, glaring.

"It's an old tape of my father's," I say. "And apparent-ly Rick Driver's."

"Where'd you get it?"

Saad meets my eyes and nods. Ted gives me the same consent.

"We found it in a box of my father's things," I say.

"Where'd this box come from?"

"Rick Driver's grandmother's house a few towns over."

"You said you didn't know where he'd been hiding."

"I didn't know, not when you asked me."

"Take me there now," he says. All the while, the sheriff has been giving me a suntan from the intensity of his glare.

"It's gone. Burned to the ground. Someone didn't want us to find it."

At this, he finally gives me a break from his heat vision and looks over at Clive. "Empty your pockets, Clive."

"What? No."

"I know I can't force you, but I swear …"

Clive reaches into his pocket and produces a mag-net the size of a hockey puck.

Sheriff Watkins takes his hat off and rakes his fin-gers over his buzz cut. "For heaven's sake, Clive."

"You know that tape could sink us!"

The sheriff takes off his hat and rubs his eyes with his thumb and forefinger. "Did I tell you to do this? Did I say burn a goddamned house down?"

I chime in. "He also assaulted Ranger Cassavetes and held us at gunpoint."

"I was just keeping an eye on them!"

"Well, Christ on a bike, Clive!" Sheriff Watkins hooks his thumbs into his belt, turns to me. "Have you watched the tape yet?"

"Not all of it," I say. "But we've seen enough."

"Then it's game over," he says, more to Clive than to me. When he speaks again, there's something soft in his voice. "Keep in mind that I was friends with your dad, and I only wanted to do right by the people of this town. We were never out to scam anyone."

He begins walking back toward the fire chief, eyes on the gravel of the parking lot. The firefighters come out of the last room in the motel and give the all-clear.

My heart is still racing; I can feel it up to my temples. "What about Clive?"

The sheriff stops and looks up at the sky as if he can see the northern lights. "I figure it's best to let that lie," he says, "unless you want to explain your own breaking and entering. There would be a lot of charges, a lot of paperwork, your ranger friend will lose his job …"

None of us can say anything to that, so we just let him walk off.

"So, can we have the power back on now?" LeDoux says to Clive, who quickly rejoins his wife and hurries back inside.

The lights come back on and the fire truck leaves. The crowd moves back inside and it's like the whole thing never happened. We're the last of the motel guests standing outside.

"Let's get this show on the road," LeDoux says.

Back in our room, Saad and Chris connect the camcorder to Saad's laptop. They push the ends of the beds together until the corners touch and a triangle is formed with the dresser. We all sit around like it's movie night, only the popcorn and pizza are missing.

The video starts with an exterior shot of Rick Driver's grandmother's house. The paint on the porch hasn't peeled away yet, the steps are in perfect working order. The screen door swings open and a leaner, younger Rick Driver walks out onto the porch.

"Don't waste the battery," he says.

"Just testing it," says the cameraman.

"Get it in the car, then grab the suits," Driver says. "We're on a schedule."

Behind Rick, through the porch's posts and the screen of the door, a smaller figure stands still, watching. The door opens slowly and a child stumbles out, not even as tall as the railing. The child nears the steps, turns, reaches up to the railing. The child smiles at the camera. The child is me.

"Let's get in the car, sweetie," the cameraman says.

"Are we making a movie?"

"You bet. It's going to be a big movie, too!"

Static overtakes the screen, then the film resumes. Leaf-covered branches brush against the passenger window of a car. Music is playing on the stereo. Sunlight adds a glow to the greenery.

"Shut that off," Driver says.

More static, then the start of the famous Roanoke Ridge footage. I've seen this a hundred times, maybe more. But this is different somehow. The adult Sasquatch is behaving the same way, moving slowly around the infant, not giving too much away. But the infant … the infant looks comical. It does not look like an animal at all. And the sound it makes —

"Nate!" the Sasquatch yells to the camera. "Get her to behave herself!"

"Damn it, Laura! What did I say?!"

The infant Sasquatch holds still, slowly sinking behind a log with half the bark missing. The film is now precisely how I remember the footage. There's a mist on the mountain that makes the costumes look greyer. The static returns.

"Wow," LeDoux says. "You're a child star."

Static continues to play. Saad's screen is like a window looking out on a snowstorm.

"There's got to be something else here," I say.

Danny LeDoux gets up and pulls his phone out of his pocket. "I'll leave you to watch the rest, then," he says, heading for the door.

Chris stands up and follows his boss to the door. He turns quickly, reaches out for the camcorder, then hesitates. "I'll come back for that," he says.

"Thank you," I say. "I owe you."

"I'll drive you home," Moira says to Ted, standing by as he stands up, ready to catch him should he stagger. She's watching Ted, maybe checking to see if his pupils are responsive. It feels like something more, though, the way her eyes drop down and linger.

Ted walks over to me and stops about a foot away. He smiles and holds me in a half hug. "For what it's worth, I know you'll make the right decision about your website," he says. His fingertips slide down my forearms as he breaks his embrace and walks out. He gets in Moira's truck, rolls the window down, and waves before driving away.

"What does he mean? What decision?" Saad asks. He looks confused, maybe even a little angry. He's trying not to be. The room seems so much larger now.

"I got an offer to sell ScienceIA," I say.

"When?"

"Last week."

"And you didn't say anything. Not to me."

"I was afraid to tell you."

"Why?" Saad asks, the purest look of confusion on his face. "You can tell me anything."

"I know. It's just — I was afraid you'd be disappointed in me. You've always been so supportive of me and the website. I didn't want you to think that I was a quitter."

Saad raises his arm like he might squeeze my shoulder, then drops it again. "I promise, I'll never think that." He steps forward and hugs me. He's never hugged me. He's always showed the poise and restraint of a British aristocrat. Even as he does it, he knows it's weird, and he steps back and stares at the carpet. "Sorry," he says.

"Don't be."

"I should call Ammi," he says.

Static and snow continue to play on Saad's laptop for minutes after everyone has left. I fast-forward through the video. Just as I'm about to give up, there's more footage of Roanoke Ridge. I quickly hit play and the video returns to normal speed.

I see my own face, over twenty years younger, wearing a riding hood sort of thing made from fur.

"Daddy, it's hot."

"We'll go get ice cream as soon as we're finished," the cameraman says.

"When?"

"Soon."

"This is going to be a beaut," Rick says. "A real beaut. We'll give old Roger Patterson a run for his money."

"I don't care about his money, I care about our money," the cameraman says. "Just make sure Watkins pays up."

EPILOGUE

I think Bigfoot is blurry, that's the problem. It's not the photographer's fault.
Bigfoot is blurry. And that's extra scary to
me, because there's a large, out-of-focus
monster roaming the countryside.

— Mitch Hedberg, *Strategic Grill
Locations*, Comedy Central, 2003

IN THE MORNING, THERE'S A KNOCK AT THE
door. Standing on the other side is Danny LeDoux,
staring down at his phone as always. "You killed my
show," he says.

"Excuse me?" I step outside, closing the door behind me.

"No Sorel, no show. It's dead, because of you and
your friend there."

He finally looks up. His face is like that of a boy,
with a look of naive innocence that almost makes me
want to forget what he just said to me.

"A man died, at the hands of someone who was like a grandfather to me, and you blame me?"

"Gotta blame someone," he says. "This is America. There's a thousand Rick Drivers out there. But Berton Sorel? He's one of a kind. And now he's sitting in a jail cell."

"You played your part, too."

"I just let you use some equipment to expose a hoax. I didn't turn Berton Sorel over to the cops. Besides, do you think any diehard squatcher cares that we got to the bottom of the Roanoke Ridge Bigfoot mystery? You watch, in a year or two people will have forgotten what we've done here. But they'll remember the video with over two million hits on YouTube. Because people believe what they want. Which is why I'm rooting for the raccoons in the upcoming battle for resources on this overcrowded planet."

"Mr. LeDoux, there are no nice words for a person like you," I say.

"Well," he says, smiling, "there's *persistent* — some people consider that a virtue. I have another proposal for you. More generous — if you can believe it — than my last offer."

"Why?"

"Frankly, Laura, you have what I want. You have the millennials. You got your hands so tight around their overeducated, underpaid throats that the bruising is starting to show. I want that. I want to feel my hands where yours are. Sure, we own older white males, and homeowners who don't foresee an increase in their personal fortunes. But only twenty-seven point two percent of our views have four plus years of college. Less than fourteen percent are white collar, professional, management. Our viewers are old, and getting older. I wouldn't sleep with them and neither should you."

"I'm not sure what I can —"

"Look at your audience. Sixty-five percent of them are college educated. You dominate the twenty-five- to thirty-four-year-olds, second strongest among eighteen- to twenty-four-year-olds. We're talking about beautiful, fit, smart, health-conscious people. You have nineteen million likes on Facebook. And my personal favourite stat, seventy-two percent of traffic to your site is done via mobile platform. NatureWorld needs to be the go-to site for mobile science content for the under-forty crowd."

"What do you want me to do?"

"Consider my offer."

"What are you offering?"

"Screw the deal with Geocomm. We'll match their offer for your website. What have they offered you, a consultant position at your own website? I wouldn't insult you. So, take the check and a month off, tan on a beach somewhere, then come work for me."

"I've invested a lot more than just time and money into my site, Danny. I've built it from pieces of my own soul. I'm not sure I can just give it up. It's who I am."

"So is your driver's licence. I hope you don't get misty every time a traffic cop asks you to give it to him. Look, we'll do one better. We'll put you in front of the camera, give you your own programming to direct and host. Take your message to a whole new demographic in a new medium. Don't you want to go out into the field?"

"What do you mean, 'into the field'?" I ask.

"You may or may not know that our big ratings come from shows with the word *monster* in it. *Ancient Monsters*, *Prehistoric Monsters*, *Monsters from the Deep*, *Hunting Monsters*. The network wants you to spin that content for your demographic, weave them into the fold."

There was a time, growing up in a house where my parents rarely spoke to each other, that I spent rainy Sundays glued to the television. The Learning Channel — which, believe it or not, is what TLC once stood for — used to run marathons of their educational programs. I grew up on *Paleoworld*, *Archaeology*, and *Connections*. Even the ads for the network tried to impart a tidbit about the Sphinx or the Napoleonic Wars. There was a feeling of discovery watching those shows, like I was always on the cusp of learning something that might change my world. More than anything, that's what I wanted to bring to people who clicked on ScienceIA.

"If I'm going to cover cryptid content," I say to Danny, "I'm going to do it honestly. If I see a coyote with mange, I'm not calling it a chupacabra. I'm definitely not calling a catfish a lake monster. Does that work for you? I'm not going to be cute and leave a mystery open for interpretation. Data dictates the results."

"We'll have to workshop that as a slogan, but I can dig it. One of our second-highest-rated programs is *Myth Breakers*. Your target demographic loves tearing down old beliefs and calling baby boomers out on their bullshit, I get that."

"Do I get to pick my team or are you going to commission focus groups to select a viewer-friendly, photogenic cabal of wholesome American archetypes?"

"You're media savvy enough to pick your own crew, but I'd like to think you'd take my suggestions under advisement. And Dr. Laidlaw will have to consult. I can't get rid of that guy. He can't stop himself from explaining things."

"In the media landscape we have today," I say, "we could use a little less concision and a little more elaboration."

"Good, then you're stuck with him."

"What's the expiration date on this offer?"

"I'd say a week is more than a reasonable shelf life for this," he says. Then he pivots away to peer down at his phone screen.

Through the gossamer curtains I can see Saad packing up the rest of his things. I know it's Saad because it can be no one else, but through the curtains, with nothing but natural light inside the room, it could be anyone or anything moving about.

ACKNOWLEDGEMENTS

This book's existence would be nothing more than speculation and blurry images if not for those who have worked so hard to advance science education and skepticism. Without the podcast *Monster Talk* and its hosts, Blake Smith and Dr. Karen Stollznow, I never would have realized the power that monsters, myths, and folklore have to advance scientific principles in an entertaining way. And though skeptical podcasts featuring scientists discussing Nessie or Bigfoot planted the seed for this novel, it was Bryan Jay Ibeas who helped me cultivate the book and Mandy Hopkins who helped to harvest it. Thanks also to my wife, Sheeza Sarfraz, who patiently listened to my wild ideas and helped focus them into a coherent plot. Without her insight and support, this book would be just another whacky idea scribbled on a scrap of paper.